# The Winter's Song

### JEANA WATTERS

ALL RIGHTS RESERVED

No part of this book may be reproduced or transmitted in any form or by any means, electronic or mechanical, including photocopying, recording, or by any information storage and retrieval system, without permission in writing from the author, except in the case of brief quotations embodied in reviews.

Publisher's Note:

This is a work of fiction. All names, characters, places, and events are the work of the author's imagination.

Any resemblance to real persons, places, or events is coincidental.

Solstice Publishing - www.solsticepublishing.com

Copyright 2017 Jeana Watters

# The Winter's Song

# Jeana Watters

**Dedication**

For Bianca: my misunderstood Shakespearean heroine, talented violist, and my companion to the Utah Shakespeare Festival every year.

# Chapter One

*"To me can life be no commodity;*
*The crown and comfort of my life, your favour,*
*I do give lost, for I do feel it gone,*
*But know not how it went."*
*-William Shakespeare*

**MonaLee**

*I* lie in bed, staring at the blurry wall. Again. Unsure of the day, the month, the week. If I look out the window, I can see which season it is—winter with its naked branches or bloom-filled spring. Or, I could turn on the television resting in the armoire, but I don't care. It's just another day in this prison.

My holding cell looks pretty, with its expensive paneling and designer moldings. I find my eyes following the pathway of the ceiling with its paneled diamonds meeting with an intricately, carved flower at each intersection. I'm in a car, waiting at this turn and then, driving around each roundabout, in hopes it will take me right out of this black hole. It would seem to most everyone I live in the lap of luxury, taking readied meals on a tray in bed. But I am a prisoner, forced to ingest whatever they put on that tray, including the pills. So many pills. Sometimes I have enough energy, or courage, to stumble over to the mahogany table by the window that overlooks the courtyard, and am brave enough to let the sunlight stream onto my face or let the wind slip through the window, *whispering of another time when I wasn't frightened of light, or wind, or what's in the next room.*

My stomach rumbles awareness that lunch will soon arrive. Just before my next meal, the medication begins to wear off, but then I'm forced to swallow my next dose. I usually have fifteen minutes to write, when I'm free and not dulled. I climb from the bed and dig out the box where I keep all my letters, and a pen. I've written her letters on and off for years, letters addressed to Perdita, my baby who died.

I was allowed to hold my daughter for mere minutes before Perdita was extricated from my swollen hands. "Babies need to be checked," the doctor had said. Of course I knew babies needed to be weighed and measured and made sure that everything was all right. But how could they have plucked my healthy baby—crying out with those lungs of hers, lungs capable of greatness someday, maybe even singing for thousands as I had done—and return to say the baby had stopped breathing?

"What are you saying?" I asked the doctor who offered those crippling words, words about breathing passages and fluids clogging airways. "Where is she?"

"The baby's gone. You shouldn't see her now," the doctor had said, with lips that seemed to move, but the words registered nothing. "You need rest."

I reached from the bed. I needed my baby, even if she wasn't breathing any longer, even if the doctor was speaking a truth I didn't then, or never quite would, comprehend. The doctor flinched from me as I yanked on his arm. "I want to hold her. I don't care what's healthy for me!"

"I'm sorry, please understand," he said, gently pushing me back toward my bed. I began to scream and howl and cry, thrashing against the sheets. I remember the struggle, but couldn't understand who had held me there on the bed, the heavy, heartless hands that kept me down. The *grasp was his. He should have loved me, not hurt me. Those were the same hands I once had longed would touch me everywhere. A shot poked my arm from behind and then blackness. I sank into a deep, bitter sleep that would attempt to erase the last eight hours of giving birth to my daughter, of the last nine months of pregnancy, as if it were just on the edge of my consciousness but never quite within my memory. The baby I was never able to hold again, or feel beneath my fingertips.*

*I couldn't cry out my loss because I was deadened, my eyes cold stones staring straight ahead. It was the "pain medication" offered at each meal by those sterile and frigid hands. Those hands setting down the tray with salads and grilled chicken but quick to pull away from me, as if I were contagious. I took those pills faithfully; for how else could I endure this life I was forced to live without my baby, without love, just without?*

*Andrew. He had been my only source of light in the many years since. I saw kindness in his dark eyes, and that got me through each day. His hands offered me fresh flowers from time to time and he would sit and actually talk to me, as if I were still alive. He was the one who secured me a pen and some paper, even though I'd not been granted those few items from the housekeepers who traipsed in and out of my room, always carefully locking the door behind them. Andrew was my husband's personal assistant. He had been his right-hand since I met Leo. Andrew knew everything. He'd been there before marriage was a jail sentence, before Perdita was a dream beyond my fingertips and all the while, when grieving became as normal to me as the trays and the hands. If I said the name Perdita, he didn't walk away as the tray ladies or housekeeper did as if I were simply talking crazy. He nodded and confirmed that yes, Perdita had existed. He knew all.*

*I love Andrew. He'd sometimes just sit on the foot of my bed, or by the chair near the bed, and let me talk or be silent, depending on how medicated I was at that moment. Just a few days ago, however, Andrew said something. Something that made me believe that maybe, just maybe, Perdita is still alive as I'd always suspected. I spoke of her eyes. When she was born, in that periphery of my memory, I tried to seek beyond the blur to the color of those little, tear-shaped eyes. They were blue. The shade of the Mediterranean Sea. That's when Andrew had said, "Yes, they're blue." He hadn't corrected himself and said "were". Instead, he just excused himself, walked to the door and hesitated a moment as if considering just another word or two, then opened the door and left. Slowly, sadly turning the lock to keep me imprisoned. That's when hope took root in my heart. It had always been there, like a waiting seed covered in earth, patient for its time to bloom in the sun, and here it was now, growing in my heart, anchoring its roots around my lungs until I could hardly breathe. Only days ago.*

*I unclasped the pen and put its inky head to the lined paper, thinking lovingly of my little girl—my very own flesh and blood—whose memory I love so deeply, but I hadn't been able to grasp onto an idea of the person she would be now. How old would Perdita be? A teenager perhaps? Seven? A young woman with a veil and hopeful flowers clasped in her hands? How many years had passed? What would she look like now? The only certainty, her blue eyes. If they hadn't outgrown that same blue all babies have, then they were my eyes, my ice blue. I focus my pen on the paper:*

*My sweet Perdita,*
*I have reason to believe you are really still here as I've always known. I will find you, I promise you that. I don't*

know how long it will take, but I will make my way to you and I will....

*\*\*\**

*a*soft knock taps on the door. I scramble to hide my letter under the covers. Andrew comes in a little more rushed than usual and sits in the chair beside my bed.

"I can't tell you where she is," he says, in a whisper. "And please don't ask me anything more, but if there's something you'd like me to give her, I will do it. I only have a couple minutes, and I can guarantee he will not know."

My body begins to shake. I'm not sure why, it probably needs its next dose of drugs. I pull the letter out from where it waits crumpled under the covers and crawl under the bed, pulling out the rest of the letters. I add my current, unfinished letter to the bottom and push them all together.

"Is this too much?"

"I'll make it work," he says, and slides the thick bunch of loose papers into the side of his suit coat.

"Why? Why now?"

He stops, but doesn't turn to me. "I shouldn't have let this happen. I'm sorry. And you should know I'm sick. I'm retiring next month." He drops his head and then leaves. I hear the hateful sound of the lock clicking.

I stare at the door. Its only job to hold me in. He knows where Perdita is! He knows how to get something to her. I must find her. But how? I know. I will hide the pills that come on the tray every meal. It will be hard; I've been drugged for so long, and my body will react like a drug addict when I try to stop. But I'll do it. I will withstand the shaking and jittering, and I will be free of the dazed existence. I must fight my way through their painful *absence. My body needs the drugs now, but I need Perdita more.*

*I will wean myself off those pills just as I'd weaned myself off the memory of my baby and accepted the death I knew couldn't be. I'm still shaking when the hands help me off the floor, into bed, and another set of hands place my lunch tray with the little paper cup cradling my pills on the table beside the bed. I nod thank you and after the door fastens, I chop off half the pill with my knife. I will search everywhere. I will scour the world until I find Perdita.*

## Chapter Two

*"When daffodils begin to peer,*
*With heigh! the doxy over the dale,*
*Why then comes in the sweet o' the year,*
*For the red blood reigns in the winter's pale."*
*-William Shakespeare*

*L*ike an abandoned toy thrown out for the dogs, the girl sat at a nearby table without so much as a sniff from the other lifties. She was taking mouse-sized nibbles from a brown bread sandwich in a quiet corner of the restaurant. Her long, dark hair hung over her shoulders as she stared into an open book. Phil wasn't sure how long she'd worked there; he'd noticed her walking to one of the lower lifts without skis or a snowboard this morning. Piper, her nametag read. It was pinned on the standard-issue tan and blue ski jacket that all the ski-life operators wore, which now dangled from the back of her chair.

Phil walked past her, toward the table closest, to the stone fireplace where his roommate Heath was inhaling a piece of pepperoni pizza. It seemed all they ate anymore was pizza; the home-cooked meals he'd left behind seemed a million miles away. He missed his mom and her food. The guys who worked at the resort restaurants—the snowboarders they spent their days off with, shredding the mountain—didn't mind slipping them a piece of pizza here or a bowlful of soup there, something that wouldn't be missed or tracked. It was an agreement they had. The lifties knew to look the other way when the kitchen workers brought friends without lift passes onto their lifts. Phil looked down at his own sausage pizza. It was just as well. Pizza would get him through another day.

Settling into the chair beside Heath, Phil said, "Best pow day since we got here."

Heath swallowed the lump of pizza he'd been working on and nodded. Then looked back at his pizza and took another mammoth bite of cheese and pepperoni.

"You starved?"

"If we hurry, we can ride the tram up and be back to our lifts by the end of lunch break," Heath said, between bites. "You in?"

Phil took a bite of his own pizza now, to buy him a couple moments with his thoughts. He looked over to the girl in the corner, then turned back to Heath. "Go without me. I need a break."

"Your loss," Heath said, then stuffed the last half of the pizza into his mouth and pulled on his beanie, coat, and gloves as he chewed, the pizza bulging out his cheeks. "Later, dude!" he shouted to Phil on his way out the door.

Phil nudged his chin to him as goodbye, then slouched down in his chair and propped his feet onto Heath's abandoned spot beside the fireplace. The fire warmed his feet despite the layers of boots and socks.

He took a careful bite and chewed. It had been snowing all morning; it could end up being the best powder day they'd had on the mountain since the beginning of November, when he and his friends started working here on ski season day one. The four of them—Heath, Zane, Tommy, and Phil—had arrived from California only the day before, moving into a two-bedroom condo in Park City, Colorado and filling most of the remaining lift-operator vacancies. Phil's father knew the owner of the resort and had secured jobs for them. His father hadn't been exactly thrilled about Phil taking a year off after only one year of college, but he'd finished his freshman year on academic probation at San Diego State and had no idea on a major.

His father had agreed that, yeah, maybe he could use a little time to regroup before officially damaging his GPA. *And Phil thought, why not in Park City where he could ride all winter long?* So he gathered a few of his more aimless buddies and packed them up in his SUV with their wrinkled clothes-stuffed duffle bags, clamped their snowboards onto the roof rack, and drove the ten hours to Park City, as simply as if they'd decided to go see a late movie.

Living there had been a lot like college, but without worrying about missing classes and falling grades. He could snowboard when he wanted. He went to work when he was supposed to because his friends were all going there too, and they could ride half the day with the appearance of work. So far, this winter had been exactly what he'd hoped for—a little respite from the stress of growing up and the responsibility that tagged along.

Phil finished his pizza and took a big swallow of soda, then surveyed the room. She was still there, bent over her book. He could go talk to her. *Why not?* It wasn't like talking to a girl was anything new. He'd had his share of girlfriends—coming and going through high school and college just like another math or English class, another mediocre grade. Some of those girls yanking him back into bed in the morning had been the cause of his low grades last year. He was already seeing a girl, another California transplant who was a surfer in the summer, snowboarder in the winter. She wore only a bra with board pants on sunny days and rode around the mountain with her cleavage enticing just about everyone and her yellow hair flashing behind her like sunrays. She did it for the attention. She worked at the snowboard rental shop, fitting people into their temporary boots and boards. Summer was her name. And summer was her thing. The snowboarding played second fiddle to her beloved surfing. She was the kind of girl whose daddy gave her enough credit cards that she spent last summer in Costa Rica in a small, surf town with a couple guys. All friends, she'd said. Maybe, maybe not. But Phil didn't really care. She was cavalier about sleeping around, cavalier about him. He didn't want a girlfriend, but she ended up at his apartment every couple of nights, waking beside him the next morning. He didn't know where she was the rest of the time and didn't think about it.

Still, this girl sitting alone before him seemed interesting. He didn't know why. Maybe because she was the anti-Summer. The Winter, he joked inwardly. As Phil stood to find out if his interest was justified, he felt his hands moisten with sweat as he gathered his things from the table and shuffled, ever so aloof, over to her table and sat. Like he owned the table or the resort.

She looked up from her book—her finger sliding between the pages to hold her place—and raised her eyebrows, waiting. Her eyes were round and so, so blue—like the ocean he missed seeing from his bedroom window back home. He was struck mute for a moment, staring into them as if their blue was stretching into her soul, able to reveal anything about her he wanted to know.

"I'm Phil. I'm a lifty, too," he said, finally. He opened his hand toward her, to shake in official greeting, he supposed, but felt strange with his outstretched hand waiting. Too formal, too much like his father.

She set her book facedown and slipped her small hand into his. They shook awkwardly. Inside his rough, weather-beaten hands, her fingers felt warm and soft. He could still feel it there after she'd taken her hand back.

"Piper," she said. She looked down at her book, which made it seem to Phil that she wished he'd just move along and leave her to her reading.

Yeah, all right, he thought and started to pick himself up off the chair.

"You don't have to go," she said. She looked up at him, and he noticed that she had freckles on her nose. He imagined playing connect-the-dot with them in bed the morning after.

"You're sure?"

She nodded, and he settled back down into the chair.

"What're you reading?"

"Jane Eyre, for my British Lit class," she said, picking up the book and flashing the cover of an English landscape. She dog-eared her page and closed the cover.

"You're a student?" he asked.

"Yeah, at the U. I commute here every other day, go to school on the others. Gotta pay the rent." She flashed him a timid smile. "What about you?"

"I'm on sabbatical," he said, offering his own charming, signature smile. The one he knew over the years had been foolproof; the girls ate it up.

Piper didn't seem to notice, though, as she was looking down at the cover of the book, pressing her hands over the paper cover where it curled up.

"You ride?" Phil asked.

She shook her head. The tips of her brown, wavy hair brushed against her shoulder. "Nah. Don't ski either. I'm just here for a job."

"You're crazy. You have a free pass hanging around your neck—a pass a million guys I know would kill for—and you don't even care."

She shrugged. "I never learned how."

"So why'd you come here?"

"A guy in my math class said he knew of a job."

"Oh," Phil said, a little bit too fast. *A guy?* "Yeah, it pays okay, I guess. But it does have this little perk—free snowboarding."

Piper pressed her hands around a Styrofoam cup, left them there for a bit like she was warming them up, then brought the cup to her lips and took a long swallow.

"You come all the way up the mountain for the coffee?" he asked.

"No, the hot chocolate. That guy in my math class, Mike, he's the one selling hot chocolate out there at that little stand. It's so good, so creamy. Reminds me of my mom's back home."

Seemed weird that Phil had just been thinking of his own mother back home and how he missed her food. "Back home?"

"Minnesota," she said. "And yes, before you ask, I came to Colorado just for school, just as I come all the way up the mountain for $8.50 an hour."

Phil raised his hands in a don't-shoot-me pose and said, "Fair enough. Well, look, I know you've gotta get back to your book and I'm gonna get a couple more runs in before it's back to the lifts, so I won't keep you."

As Phil stood to leave, he looked around. The restaurant had filled since he'd been sitting there and he hadn't seemed to notice the people filtering in and out. But she was just another girl who he'd just had an ordinary conversation with. Nothing special. He wondered if it'd be too forward to offer to teach her to ride. *Would it be too much?* Yeah, probably. Phil didn't know why he was still thinking about her as he made his way out the door and pulled his board from its resting place, sandwiched between other waiting snowboards and skis whose owners were lunching. She was kind of pretty—no prettier than other girls he'd had—and their conversation had been unremarkable. Phil shrugged the remaining thoughts of her off as he strapped his booted feet into the bindings and coasted down the hill to the lift that would take him up the spine of the mountain.

\*\*\*

*S*everal hours later, dusk settled in, turning the snow-covered hill a pearly pink and jagged gray from the shade thrown off the pine trees—like the insides of seashells Phil collected from the sandy beaches of his childhood. It was closing time. Phil rode down the mountain at full speed, the icy layer of snow having re-frozen after an eager, afternoon sun tried its best to melt the snow away. Phil let his mind remain empty as his board carved back and forth, back and forth, like chalk etchings on a blank slate. His headphones pounded racing drumbeats and hurried words of old-school punk music into his ears.

    Yes, this was why he was here—to forget everything. His father's expectations had weighed on him last year, like mounds of snow about to be upset. And the avalanche would have happened had he not fled from there—from his father's incessant encouragement to get his grades up, major in business, and get his MBA so he could take over the family's financial investment company someday. Yes, he knew how *lucky* he was. His father had told him over and over again that his career was set out for him like the clothes his mom used to place so carefully on his chair, the night before school, as a child. So lucky, he thought, slipping down even faster on the slick ice. The metal fringe of his board scraped so hard into the ice he could hear it over his music. It wasn't until he caught an edge and slammed onto his back and then back over, landing surprisingly onto his board again without skipping a beat, that he shifted down to a slower sped. But he kept right on riding and looked around to see if anyone else had seen his impressive fall and recovery. Only a group of ski patrollers were moving in the distance above him, too far away to notice. But something wasn't right. A sharp pain coursed through his left arm. He must have twisted it under him as he fell. He held onto his elbow, just to give himself a little support, as he kept riding.

Phil knew he'd have to go back to school next year, finish college and hopefully land on his feet by the end of it all. Then, maybe, he could be the son his father expected him to be. But, for now, he didn't want to think about it. His arm was throbbing. *Great*, he thought. *What's wrong with it?*

Phil slid to the lift-operator lodge, had a bit of difficulty getting his boots out of the bindings, then left his snowboard leaning against the rack and went in to gather his things. Inside, a couple of people were rummaging through their lockers. Piper was there. He recognized her wavy hair, a bit tousled, like that beach, sun-dried wave he liked on Summer. Phil walked past and pulled his bag from the locker, yanked off his gloves and headphones and shoved them inside his bag, all with one hand, and then traded his work coat for his own snowboarding jacket. Heath, Zane, and Tommy swept in a couple minutes later and Phil waited for them, trying not to notice Piper leaving. She was hugging that same book into her chest. He shook his head. Reading when she could be snowboarding.

The guys piled into Phil's Pathfinder, and headed out of the bumpy, snow-pocked parking lot. Phil kept his arm cradled in his lap, but the bumpy ride caused his arm to jerk up and down. He tried to ignore the pain. He bent over, trying to wedge his arm and the accompanying pain inside the hollow his stomach made, but that hurt too. And the pain was increasing.

"What're you doing?" Zane asked, from the passenger seat.

"I took a fall on the way down," Phil said, lifting his weak limb that bent over at the wrist like a baby who couldn't support its own head. "My arm's killing me." Then Phil tucked it back against his middle.

"Dude," Heath said, from the back seat. "What if it's broke?"

"It's not broken," Phil said. "It can't be."

If it weren't for being cooped up in a six hundred square foot hole with three other guys, he would have been rocking back and forth in fetal position, his whole body wrapped around his throbbing arm. But he'd had to try to act like it didn't bother him while it stung and pulsated and hung at his side. Finally, he couldn't take it anymore and asked Heath to take him to the late hour's clinic.

After a little paperwork, a discussion with a bearded, white-haired doctor as friendly and charming as Santa Claus, bandages wrapped around his arm like a baby swaddled in a blanket, and a bottle of OxyContin rattling in his pocket, Phil felt better.

"Your arm's not broken," the doctor had said, tucking Phil's arm into a sling. "But it's sprained. Badly sprained."

"I'm so glad it's not broken. Too much snowboarding to be done," he said, aware of the OxyContin stealing some of his pain.

"Oh, there will be no snowboarding," he said, smiling so jolly it was misleading, like Santa saying through his rosy cheeks that he's been naughty this year.

"There has to be snowboarding," Phil said.

"Not for two weeks there won't be," he said, his twinkling eyes serious.

Phil threw his head back in dismay. "But I'm a lifty."

"Yeah, you really shouldn't be lifting anything with that arm either," Dr. Claus said. "Especially a snow shovel."

No snowboarding, no shoveling—he'd be useless. He wondered if he'd still be able to work. Phil explained the situation to his boss, who was understanding, saying he could work the lower lifts and stick to walking when he should be riding. Despite the gratification of the daily companionship of OxyContin, Phil was feeling down. With nothing else to do at lunch, he may even feel desperate enough to ask Piper to borrow a book.

Phil was downgraded to Snow Hare, the kiddie lift at the bottom of the mountain, just right outside the lifty locker room. The lift crept up the mountain like a child's train set, dropping off its toddlers and first-timers at the top of the hill, then crept back down the mountain to pick up a new gang of unsure gliders. Piper was shoveling last night's snow dusting off the "Please Load Here" sign when Phil approached.

"Hey," he said to her and shrugged off his backpack into the shack's open door.

"Hello, again," she said, stopping a moment and then resuming her shoveling. She wore a knitted blue and green hat with a pom-pom at the top and earflaps. "You lost?"

Phil shook his head and held up his sling, opting for silence.

"I'm sorry. What happened?" Piper propped her shovel up against the shack and came closer. Close enough that he could see straight into her eyes, all blue as a clear morning.

"I fell coming down the mountain last night."

Piper held her head sideways. "Ouch! Is it broken?"

"No, just sprained. But bad enough that I can't snowboard for a coupl'a weeks."

"Ahh, I see. So you're stuck down here," Piper said. She smiled this smile, her top lip curved up like a Cupid's bow. "It's not so bad."

At that, a ski instructor skied over with a trail of ducklings waddling behind him on their little skis. Piper stood by and helped them waddle to the right place, guided them onto their conveyor-belt ride up the mountain, scooping up fallen ducklings and depositing them onto the lift seats.

"Look, Phil, why don't you come over here and help the kiddos on the lift, and I'll do the heavy lifting and the shoveling," Piper said. "You're not too debilitated to do that, right?"

"I can do that," he said, and shuffled over to where Piper had been standing.

It was a slow morning, just the ski school and a couple of stragglers passing through their gate. Snow started falling, furious and dizzying, and the day turned cold. The kind of cold that makes your bones ache. They both retreated into the heated shack and watched to see when people were coming to check their tickets and help them onto the lift.

"The ramp's shoveled, for now, so we can take turns going out into the snow," Piper said, watching out the window and rubbing her gloveless hands near the heating vent.

This girl was nice. She was pretty and sweet in a Heidi-with-braids sort of way. Phil slid down the side of the shack near the vent. Still, he couldn't get over the fact that she preferred reading to riding and didn't care to do anything about it. This made Phil crazy. Maybe he'd give her one more chance.

"You ever thought about learning to ride?" he asked.

"Nah," Piper said. "No money, no skis, no board."

"I could teach you, you know?"

Piper raised her eyebrows. "Really?"

"Not to ski. I don't do that. But if you wanna learn to snowboard, I'm your guy."

"Well," she said, hesitating and then shrugging. "I don't see any harm in it."

"No, no," Phil smiled up at her with his signature grin again. "No harm in that. After all, we are already on the bunny slope. I don't think my doctor would object to this sort of backyard hill." *Or would he?* Whatever.

Just before lunch break, Phil walked the three paces to the lifty lodge and Hank allowed him to rifle through the old, storage closet full of things left, forgotten, and unwanted. Just as he thought, he remembered seeing an old K-2, flat-tailed snowboard—purple and yellow and all firecracker designs—laying and ignored beside discarded jackets, hats, mismatched gloves, and thrashed bags. Phil pulled it out and dusted off the dirt and cobwebs with his good hand. The bindings were small so she could use them with whatever snow boots she was already wearing. With optimism, Phil grabbed his own board, plunked them both side-by-side before Piper who was standing at the Snow Hare shack.

"Your first lesson's today."

Phil negotiated with one of the lifties from a nearby lift to come over and cover for them so they could take their break at the same time. They rode up the lift together, Phil trying to be patient as the lift putted up the hill.

"You're sure your doctor's okay with this?" Piper asked, as she watched him hook his free boot under the snowboard dangling from his other boot and tried to do the same with hers.

He nodded. "I'll be careful."

"Just don't go trying to keep me from falling," she said, and stared off into the light, airy snowflakes like feathers floating down. She stuck out her tongue until a snowflake landed, then reeled it in and closed her mouth.

She's like a kid, he thought. He had brought the board over to her just minutes before and helped her bind in her snow boots—seriously, they were child-sized Sorel's, she'd told him she'd gotten them cheaper in the child size. The flat tail made her ride regular, so he didn't even bother doing the "push" test to see if she was goofy-footed and should be riding with the other leg forward. Beggers can't be choosers, he thought, echoing the words his mom repeated to him his entire childhood. He missed his mom, despite the clichéd advice that had stuck with him.

Her left foot locked in the binding, she limped over to the lift with her right leg, holding on to his good arm, pulling the foot stuck to the board behind her like a prisoner dragging a ball and chain. They'd gotten on the lift easily enough, but getting off was a little trickier. They were approaching the top shack at a snail's pace.

"Just park your free boot onto that pad right there," he said, pointing to the rubber rectangle between the bindings. "Then just coast down the hill like you're sledding."

"I don't sled standing up."

"Not yet," he said, and scooted to the edge of the seat. "But you will. You have to balance."

When they hit the top of the slope, Phil said, "Now." Then he placed his free boot onto the footpad and slid down as easy as if he were on a toddler slide. Phil watched Piper as he glided. She was leaning back too far, following behind her board and boots until she couldn't stand any longer and fell onto her back, shimmying down the small incline. She'd reached out for him before she fell and he could see her pull back her gloved hand, to keep from pulling him down.

She was lying in a lump at the bottom of the decline and Winnie, the upper lift operator, clamped her hand over the stop button to bring the lift to a halt.

"You okay, Piper?"

"I've seen those kiddos fall up here over and over again," Piper yelled over, with a smile and not even attempting to pull herself up yet. "You'd think I'd at least know what not to do, but here I am."

"There you are," Phil said, and he held out his own gloved hand toward her, then yanked her up. "Next time, you can hold onto me, and I'll steady you."

"What if I pull you down?"

"You won't." Charming signature smile again.

They sat together while Phil secured his other boot into the bindings, then crawled over to help Piper. He secured her boot firmly inside and said, "It's gotta be tight, so your ankles won't wobble and make you fall."

"Okay," Piper said, as she pushed herself up to standing on top of her board. "So, what now?"

"Go down just like that, on your heel side. Dig your heels in when you need to slow down," Phil said. "Oh, and try not to fall." He turned and skidded off, making his way down the hill, to show her how. Gliding back and forth between his front side and back, carving a long rope of ric-rac in the snow. He stopped after a couple S-turns and looked back. Piper was still standing where he'd left her. "You coming?"

"I'm scared," she shouted down to him.

"Okay, you're gonna fall. Just get it over with."

"Okay," Piper shouted, her voice unsteady. She began scooting on her board, a couple inches, then stopped, a couple more inches, then stopped. It wasn't until the trail of toddlers on skis followed their instructor in a semi-circle path around her that she finally built up a little speed, then fell hard.

Phil tried to scoot back up to her. "You can't be so afraid. Just go for it."

Piper nodded okay and continued her snail's pace down the mountain, now more cautious than ever. This was gonna take forever. Phil just sat and watched, then rode down the rest of the way and rode the lift back up.

When she was halfway down the hill, he came up fast from behind and sprayed snow on her in jest. The way he and his friends did to each other. But as the snow was landing on top of Piper's hat and actually seemed to push her over again, he felt bad. She was as secure as a feather on the snow. He should have known. She rolled over and sat.

"You're not a nice person," she said.

Phil couldn't tell whether she was joking or not. Phil plopped down beside her, their snowboards kissing. He began brushing the snow from her face and hat with his good hand and she looked toward him, frustrated. He had gone too far. He wanted to make her laugh. He wanted her to realize how lucky she was for the free lesson. He wanted her to want to kiss him.

"I'm sorry."

He could tell she was exasperated. "I just want to get down to the bottom. This isn't fun."

He took both gloved hands and pulled up at the edges of her cheeks, trying to force her to smile. Finally, he could see her smile breaking through the pout.

"I'll tell you what. I'll get you down the hill. A little faster than this. Do you trust me?"

She shook her head. "No, as a matter of fact, I don't."

"Come on, Piper," he said, and gave her a puppy dog look that always worked on girls. "Will you trust me?"

Piper hesitated and eyed him. She just cocked her head and waited. "Well?"

Phil slid around and began unbinding Piper's feet from the snowboard. "This is really just a narrow sled." Phil unbound his own feet and put the two snowboards side-by-side, then sat upon them, behind the first binding. "Climb aboard."

"You're kidding," she said, shaking her head and slipping herself onto the snowboards behind the second binding.

"You better hold on," Phil said, as he propelled them forward by scooting his boot on the snow. "I have no way of steering."

Good thing there were so few people on the hill. They slid down, her hands cinching him around the waist, which he liked. Halfway down, one of the snowboards began shifting the other direction.

"Lean to the right," he shouted. "We're sacrificing the K-2."

"We're both going to die," Piper shouted, and leaned closer to him. If he didn't already know it was impossible, he could have sworn she said that with a smile.

The purple board veered off to the left, and Phil and Piper sped on ahead toward their lift shack, Piper gripping tighter around Phil's waist. He could feel the warm mist of her breath on his neck. They were nearing the bottom. Phil cradled his hurt arm to his chest and used his boot to try to stop them. At the first touch of his foot to the snow, the board swung around 360 degrees, and they finally landed in a pile of coats and boards and bones against the back of the lift shack, Piper up against the wall and Phil landing in her lap, his hurt arm wedged underneath the board. Piper's hat was askew, the big pom-pom hanging down by her chin. Piper looked down at him.

"Are you all right?" she asked.

"Not quite," he answered, pulling his arm from under the board like a dead animal. "You?"

"I don't think I'm broken. The bindings are under my back though," she said, and shifted herself off the board and pushed it to the side. "Did you snap your arm?"

"I don't think so," he said. "But it hurts like a mother. I think I need another pill."

"I'm sorry about your arm," Piper looked at him wearily. "But the 'trusting you' part is not really happening."

Phil reached up with his good arm and tugged at her pom-pom. Her hat slid off her head, exposing wavy hair that had frizzed up underneath the hat. He could see what she probably looked like if he were waking up next to her in the morning. Piper reached over for the hat that Phil held to tug it back. She gave him a severe look as if warning him he didn't want to play this game with her.

"Fine," he said, and released his hold on the yarn pom-pom. "I guess this concludes our lesson until tomorrow." Phil stood and held out his hand to help Piper up. She'd already placed the hat back onto her head.

She eyed his outstretched, gloved hand warily and shook her head. "No way."

"Oh, come on. You can't tell me that wasn't fun."

Piper still shook her head, slowly, back and forth, her pom-pom following suit.

"It's more fun than reading a book," Phil said, trying to bring his point across in terms she would get.

"I disagree, and *reading a book* is a lot less dangerous." Piper grabbed onto Phil's hand, and he pulled her to standing. "I'll tell you what. I'll willingly lock myself into that deathtrap again *after* you've read Jane Eyre."

She turned to leave. Phil grabbed onto his snowboard, pulled it upright against him, and watched her walk away.

## Chapter Three

*"I have heard (but not believ'd)*
*the spirits o' the dead may walk again:*
*. . . for ne'er was dream so like a waking.*
*To me comes a creature,*
*Sometimes her head on one side, some another;*
*I never saw a vessel of like sorrow,*
*So fill'd and so becoming: in pure white robes,*
*Like very sanctity, she did approach."*
-William Shakespeare

*P*iper arched her back as she drove down the mountain into the valley, stretching her aching muscles. She shifted the car into neutral and coasted, to save on gas, and flexed her feet. She never even knew most of these muscles existed—or that she had never used them—until after she tried to get down the hill on a snowboard with Phil earlier that day.

She looked in the side mirror. The blue of her car appeared gray since it hadn't seen soap in at least three months. There was no use washing it. With as much as she drove up the mountain to Park City, it'd just get dirty again in the snow anyway. Plus, she didn't have any spare money for carwashes.

Classical music played on the radio, framing her thoughts as she drove. She didn't understand what interest that guy Phil had in her anyway. *What did he care if she didn't snowboard?* He acted as though it was a personal affront to him that she'd rather not.

Although he *was* cute, too cute. Maybe it was the dimple in his chin. Or the way his cheek kind of sunk down in his jaw that made him look chiseled. Or maybe it was his deep, brown eyes set against his blond hair—really almost golden against all that brilliant, white snow around him—that kind of just stood up on end, like he had always just taken off a beanie, which he probably had. Or his perfectly straight nose. Whatever it was, Piper chided herself to stop thinking about him and his hotness. She wished her thoughts wouldn't take her back to him. *What did it matter anyway?*

He knew how good looking he was. That's what bothered Piper most. She knew his type. And she wasn't going to play his little game and swoon like he expected her to. He'd picked the wrong girl. She wasn't the swooning type. In fact, she'd spent her entire childhood pining after one guy, John Bersani, without ever uttering a word. Just a couple stolen glances and an unfulfilled heart.

Anyway, Piper had more important things to worry about. She had just begun another semester at the U and was carrying eighteen credits. She was majoring in accounting, at her father's request, and minoring in English to give herself a treat, kind of like dessert after dinner. She'd smashed all her classes into three days so she could work Tuesdays, Thursdays, and weekends at the resort. Tomorrow, on her nineteenth birthday, she had a ten page paper due, nine pages of which she had not yet written, on George Eliot's *Middlemarch*.

Half an hour later, Piper pulled in to the driveway of her apartment building, a once majestic, old house dissected into studio apartments. Her wheels crunched over fall's leftover leaves encrusted with snow on the rocky driveway. She parked her car and made her way to the back entrance to her apartment, fitted her key into the door, and entered. As she slid through the door, her cats mewed their disapproval.

"I'm sorry, girls," she said, kneeling down to pet them both. "You know I have to work all weekend. It's the only way."

Piper kissed Mopsa squarely on her orange and white forehead, then brushed some fur off her nose. That cat's long hair was always leaving a trail. Even with only three legs, she sure seemed to get everywhere. Dorcas—her Siamese mix, blue-eyed cat—came forward for her own bit of attention. She purred and rubbed her whiskers up against Piper's cold cheek. Piper petted Dorcas from her head right down to her tail, following the bump of Dorcas's belly. It was amazing this was the same starving, fur-and-bones cat she'd picked up from The Humane Society only months before.

"Have you been eating all of Mopsa's food again?" Piper asked as she went to the silver food dishes, both as empty as oysters plucked of their pearls. The cats waited expectantly while she filled their bowls with food and topped off their water. "Yes, I'm here to serve you. Bon appetite!"

Piper deposited her backpack onto the table to pick up the phone and saw the package from yesterday still sitting unopened on her table. She knew what it was. The size and shape of the paper-wrapped package was unmistakable, but she wasn't ready for it yet. She'd felt betrayed by music, which had once brought beauty and joy into her life. But she'd decided to leave it behind. She had thought often of her viola sitting silent in its velvet case back home, like leaving behind a best friend, and missed hearing its singing voice, the familiar feel of the warm wood in her palm and against her neck, and the soothing effect it had on her when anger or frustration came. No, she still wasn't ready.

She looked past the package to the waiting phone with its red blinking light. Her mom always called on Sunday afternoon. She pressed the button.

*Piper, honey, it's Mom. I suppose you're at work again. You're never home. Call tonight when you get home. I love you!*

"I love you too," Piper said, to the voice over the answering machine and picked up the phone, the beeps of her dialing caused a momentary pause from the feasting cats.

"It's me," Piper said, upon hearing her mother's familiar phone greeting. After discussing in detail the weather in Minnesota, a high school play in which her little brother Clint had a small part, and how her mother's sewing business was going, her mother brought up the subject Piper dreaded. It was as if orchestra auditions were underlined and kissed by exclamation points on a pad of paper her mom kept near the phone.

"Yes, yes," Piper responded. "I know auditions are in the spring, but I'm not going to do it. Nothing's changed."

"Honey, maybe—"

"Mom, they tore me to pieces last year. I can't do it. I haven't even played since then." Piper sighed and continued, "Why did you send it?"

"Oh, Piper. Send what?"

"The viola. I got the package. It's sitting here on my table. Just because it's here doesn't mean I'm going to play it."

"When you're ready," her mother said, seeming suddenly resigned. "Happy birthday, Piper. I love you so much."

"I love you too, Mom."

"Oh, and Piper. I hope you haven't forgotten how to play."

"I won't forget, mom. It's like riding a bike," Piper said, although she wasn't so sure about that.

"Goodbye, Piper."

"Bye." Piper remained sitting at the table, staring over at the wrapped package, wondering how it would feel to just take it out of its case and hold it near.

She'd once loved playing. But during the audition last spring, when her parents had spent the little money they had to fly her out to the college, the panel had been relentless. When asked how long she'd taken private lessons, she'd been honest.

"I never took private lessons, but my orchestra director took me under her wing." After she began playing, a woman asked her about her *peculiar* bow grip and tried to correct the way she held the neck of the viola. Then they just dismissed her as if she were a street performer not worthy of their penny. As if her music didn't have the same beauty because she'd been taught in her school orchestra instead of with a private instructor. *What did that matter?* Maybe her technique wasn't perfect, but most people could overlook that when they heard her play. These panelists couldn't see past her fingers gripping the bow, and it had stung Piper and made her feel foolish.

She hadn't really given herself other options for college. The U was the best place for viola studies and it was the only place she'd applied, so sure she was that it would all work out. She switched her major from the music department and did the practical thing that her father had encouraged—she'd major in accounting. She couldn't bear to even pick up her viola after that. It brought tears to her eyes just thinking about the way it had felt to be dismissed like that.

So Piper just stopped cold turkey. It felt like breaking an addiction. She'd always been *the musician,* and now she wasn't. She was just another ordinary, backpack-clad girl walking along the sidewalk to class. And then she didn't get the scholarship being selected for the orchestra would have provided. That's why she'd had to get the job at the resort. She simply didn't have the money. And she was already paying less for this three hundred square foot studio apartment, owned by a cousin of her father's, than she would have at the dorms.

Although she felt herself drawn to the viola, especially when she felt her life was spinning out of her control, and its now-silent beauty, she still felt betrayed by it. A piece of her had been missing ever since. She shook her head. No, she wasn't ready yet.

Two hours later, Piper sat in her bed, tucked in the bay window of her apartment, with her notebooks sprawled out and her laptop glowing before her. The laptop had been a parting gift from her father. He shouldn't have done it. It was way more than her parents had to spend on her, but he'd given it to her, with his eyes shining and it meant the world to Piper. Comfortably dressed in plaid, flannel pajamas, Piper put the finishing touches on her paper. Piper relished writing these papers, feeling her fingers tapping on the laptop's keys like the rhythmic lull of music, and focused as much of her attention as possible on her English classes.

Her cats were curled up on the blankets around her. Dorcas awoke and watched Piper as she slid from the bed and began tidying up around the apartment.

After filling up a glass of water, she stood and looked at the package on the table. She'd left yesterday's mail next to the package and started rummaging through it. A couple of utility bills and a baby blue envelope showing her parent's return address. She opened the enveloped and sure enough, it was a birthday card with a check for fifty dollars and a short note from her mother about missing her while she was away. A short but thoughtful note from her father wished her happiness from afar. "Happy Birthday! Your brother, Clint" was scribbled over to the edge.

She looked up at the clock on the wall; it was 9:30 p.m. She sat down at the small dining table and scooted the package toward her. Maybe she'd take just one peek. Piper began carefully sliding her index finger through the brown paper, then started ripping. As she slid open the paper, she was surprised to see the case was a rich brown leather, not black cloth. This wasn't the viola she'd left behind. Intrigued, Piper clicked the latch and opened the case. Inside sat a caramel-colored viola. It was glowing.

She looked over the viola, sleeping in a bed of blue velvet like a beautiful, abandoned woman. The deep chestnut wood's dull glaze reflected the light from the antique, crystal chandelier above. Piper pulled the viola from its case and let her fingers travel over its silken, wood varnish. She'd just pluck one string. The perfect pitch of the A key rang through her apartment, like a whimper, begging. She felt a yearning in her heart. She looked to the clock. A few minutes remained before the apartment-mandated quiet time. She set the viola on the table and pulled the bow from the case and pulled open the side compartment and pulled out a circle of rosin. She began pushing the bow against the rosin back and forth absentmindedly. Both cats had jumped from the bed and were sitting by her feet, watching her with interest. Mopsa soon grew bored and began licking her paws and swiping them behind her ear. Piper stood and lifted the viola to her chin. It was so familiar, like a hug from a long lost friend, and Piper began pulling a simple scale from its strings. It was slightly out of tune so she adjusted the pegs until the strings rang out.

Piper stood and played a slow, melancholy melody she'd been writing for years that would never quite leave her head. This song was never finished. In fact, she couldn't remember when it started. Although she had a whole binder full of her compositions, this song was her mom's favorite, one she had raved on and on about. She'd been so proud of "Piper, the composer," as she liked to spout to anyone who would listen. Quite a marvel, her mom would say, considering the lack of musical ability she herself possessed. She told Piper she possessed a gift. When Piper lured the deep notes from the viola, she lost awareness of time or any problems surrounding her. At night, since she began playing in elementary school, melodies would come to her in her sleep.

Piper was eight when her father had brought home her first little viola. It was a beat up, old thing with dings and scratches in the veneer. Specifically, there was a B deliberately carved onto the front. Half of the bow's strings were splintered off at the edges. She'd wanted to play the violin, but her father knew of someone at work whose kid had been in the orchestra and had a viola for sale cheap. "It looks just the same as a violin," he had said. "It just plays a little lower."

Piper wasn't one to complain. She was always a shy, quiet girl. She'd always let everyone else talk while she sat and listened. She was listening when her friend Meg had gone on and on about how they were going to be in the orchestra and play violins together and share a music stand. Well, it hadn't quite worked out that way. Piper couldn't remember what had happened to her friend Meg from third grade. She hadn't lasted long in orchestra, she knew that much.

From the moment Piper put the bow to the beat up viola's strings, she felt something extraordinary, as if she were taken away to some place where beauty was intangible but filled the air around her, kind of like smoke.

As a child, she toted that curved, wooden stringed toy around the house with her everywhere. Like a stuffed puppy or a much-loved doll. Music was a jewel underneath her viola's shoddy façade. She even slept with her arms cradling it. That way, when the melodies came to her in her dreams, she only had to pick up the sleeping instrument and wake it with the tune she held captive in her head until it sounded out into the darkness. Sometimes, the melodies were frightening, always a little sad, always in a minor key.

One of her parents would stumble through the dark house into her room, sit on her bed, and say, "Piper, you've got to sleep. That can wait."

"But it can't," she'd say, shaking her head, the ready tears in her eyes like the melody that just had to be released onto the page. "The song will be gone in the morning."

That was when her mother bought her a notebook of lined staff paper as well as some earplugs for both herself and her father.

***

*B*ack at her apartment, Piper smiled while she played at the thought of herself so young and happy with her flaxen curls and scrawny arms and legs and remembered feeling completely loved. Always completely loved. Both cats watched her from the bed attentively—their eyes shifting back and forth with the tip of the bow—as she worked through the piece. Piper looked over to her cats. "What'cha think?"

Dorcas meowed her approval, while Mopsa bathed her legs and tail.

The acoustics in Piper's apartment were amazing—what with the ten-foot ceilings, old paneled walls and wooden floors—and made the voice from the strings cry clearly and pure.

Piper went to the pocket on the front of the viola case in hopes that there would be some sheet music stuffed away in there, something she could play now, from all the stuff she'd left behind. She struggled with the zipper and wondered exactly how much music had her mother stuffed in there. *All of it?* After some time, she was able to force the pocket open and pulled out a thick stack of paper. It wasn't what she expected—instead of staffs and black notes, there were letters and words and tons of them. All addressed to someone named Perdita. She flipped through the pages. Yes, every last one of them was meant to go to this person—Perdita. Piper felt intrusive and laid the pages on the table. They must have been left in the case by the previous owner. She'd have to call her mother tomorrow and inquire about whose letters they were so they could be returned.

Piper placed the viola back in its case and readied herself for bed. She turned out the light and knelt near the bed to say a prayer.

Piper prayed for survival in a world on her own, which was the same prayer she issued each night from her bedside. She was thankful for yet another night. Tonight she was twice as thankful, remembering back upon the reckless sled ride down the mountain with Phil. She pictured his eyes again, the way he smiled at her in his smug way. He really *was* cute. Right. Back on track. She prayed for her parents back home and her brother. And for her cats, so they wouldn't be too lonely while she was away so much. She prayed for the paper she finished and other classes. And she issued a quick thank you for bringing music back into her life and the golden instrument resting not far from her. As she uttered her amen, she stretched her legs and back one final time—her muscles were going to ache twofold in the morning, she knew—and slipped onto her back, shifting Mopsa off her pillow and turning it over before lying her head down on its cool side.

Piper lay still, listening to the cars swishing by on the busy street outside, until at last sleep came. In her dream, the woman visited again. She was always frantic, restless, searching for something. This time, Piper was in a clothing store, browsing through some racks of t-shirts in an organized rainbow of colors, when she saw her. Her unkempt, dark hair and troubled blue eyes were the same she'd seen since she was a child. She was dressed impeccably, as usual, in some shiny expensive, draping white fabric, and she always wore heels. The woman's purse fell to the ground with a thud.

"It was right here, right here!" the woman shouted, at the purse.

No one listened. The cashier at the front was checking someone out and didn't look over, as if she couldn't even hear the woman. None of the other shoppers in the store looked up, just kept their heads straight ahead and continued searching through the clothing on the racks, like robots. The store seemed to stretch deeper since she'd first walked in. She couldn't see where it ended; it just seemed to go on and on, like mirrors extending forever.

Piper rushed to the woman. "What is it? What did you lose?" she asked.

The woman's purse had spilled out onto the floor and all its contents were lying in a heap. Piper fell to her knees and began scooping up the tubes of lipstick and crumpled, paper receipts and bottles of pills and hard candy, depositing them back into her white, patent-leather purse. Behind her, the woman moaned helplessly, tears streaming down her face as Piper cleaned up her things.

"Can I help you find what you've lost?" Piper asked, again.

"No," the woman screamed, with increasing volume. "No one can help me. It's gone. Don't you see? It's gone! I can never have it back!"

The woman fell to the ground, curling into fetal position on the hard dirty floor, crying sobs that were shifting in tune to create a melody—a sad, hopeless, familiar song.

Piper woke with a start, the melody—a continuation of the sad song she'd played earlier—ringing in her head. She wasn't sure whether the woman had brought the song to her or if her playing the song on her viola earlier in the evening had summoned the helpless woman to her dream. But now she knew how to continue the piece where she'd left off. She sat up, switched on the bed-side lamp, and pulled a notebook from her nightstand, and drew a staff onto it so that she wouldn't lose the string of notes. She wished she could pull out her instrument to bring it back to life, even as the dream faded, but she had to settle for etching the notes onto paper as she couldn't wake the other tenants.

It had been so long since she'd been visited by the strange lady in her dreams. So long. But here she was again. And now her song could continue and grow.

After sketching out the notes for several lines, Piper pulled back the curtain from the window and stared out into the abandoned, cold street. A lamp was shining on the corner. She focused her eyes on the light and played the dream back in her head. Piper didn't know who the woman was. She had never seen her face in real life, only in dreams. She was the searching woman, looking for something she was resigned to never find. Piper didn't understand why *this woman* haunted her. *What did she have to do with her?* Piper always tried to help her in the dreams, but the woman wouldn't let her. And she never told Piper what it was she was looking for.

In her wakefulness, Piper was jarred thinking back to the strange pile of letters on her table. Maybe she'd read just one—so that she could find enough clues to get these letters back into the hands of this Perdita, where they belonged. Piper was humming the sad song as she went to the table and brought the letters back to her bed.

## Chapter Four

*"How will this grieve you,
When you shall come to clearer knowledge, that
You thus have publish'd me! Gentle my lord,
You scarce can right me thoroughly, then, to say
You did mistake."
-William Shakespeare*

September 7, 1981

My little Perdita,

𝒫lease don't hate me for giving you the name Perdita. It may sound strange, but it was my grandmother's name. I never knew her—she died before I was born—but my mother told me of all the wonderful things she did, how brave she was traveling from Sicily to the U.S. as a teenage girl, by herself, all alone on a boat. Mom even sang me the sweet, Italian songs her mother used to sing to her as a girl. You are honored to carry her name. I'm going to pass along her stories to you. About the rocking of the boat and the boy she met on her way over. I hope you will appreciate the name after the kids stop snickering and teasing you on the playground. Just hold your head high, my dear.

You are just months away from being born. I simply cannot wait to hold you in my arms. I've always wanted to be a mother. I married a man I truly love, and I wanted to have his baby. I put my singing career on hold for you, waiting for you. I'm worried now about when you arrive, everything won't be as I'd hoped. Sometimes, you just can't plan your life as much as you try. You'll figure that out someday, just as I have.

I'm afraid for my safety. I've done nothing wrong, but I'm in exile, hiding in an old friend's apartment. I need you to know something: Your father is a good man. I fell in love with him because he loved so completely. He loved me, he loved you when I told him you were growing inside me, and he loves what he does although being in the public eye like this is hard on him. It's hard on both of us.

Many months ago, a friend of your father's came to stay with us for an extended period of time. His name is Paul. They were roommates in prep school. I know, it sounds archaic, but your father comes from a long line of politicians and he was being molded to become another in that line and had to have the *finest schooling*. Paul had some business here in D.C., so your father offered up our place indefinitely. It would be like old times, and the two of them had a ton of catching up to do, he'd said. I didn't mind at all. Toward the end, I wasn't performing as much as usual—my tours were winding down the more pregnant I became and let's face it, no one wants to pay that kind of money to see a pregnant woman sing. Although that gives new meaning to hearing the fat lady sing.

People had warned me about this—that having a baby takes a toll on your career. I accepted that and still chose you. Baby blankets, burp rags. Suffice it to say, I'm pretty sure I've been forgotten already. There will always be another girl who can sing. I'm just a fleeting impression on the audience's ears. So, for now, my life is for you. My voice is dedicated now to singing you lullabies. I sing to you every night and morning. I hope you can hear me. I think you can.

    Why your father thinks you aren't his baby baffles me. I was never unfaithful. He'd been working so much and Paul was here, so whenever he'd come home, I'd be sitting in the living room talking with Paul. That's when your father started acting differently, more distant. Like he suspected something. But I never betrayed him. I was merely being a host to your father's friend, as I thought he would have me do. *What should I have done?* Most of our discussions were about you and the beautiful idea of you and about his own baby boy at home with his wife. He missed his little boy so much. Even in your father's absence, hearing Paul speak so tenderly of his own child made me love your father more because I knew he would feel the same way, that he would love you just like that when you arrived.

    One night, your father lost control. The stress from his campaign must have pushed him over the edge. He's up for election again this year. *Tick, tick, tick.* When he returned home from work, I was sitting rather near to Paul. His wife had sent him some recent photos of his baby—he was telling me how quickly they grow in the first year—so I had scooted over to look at them with him. Perhaps my leg was pressing against his. If it was, I didn't realize it. Yes, I felt I had once been beautiful. Men had always commented on my deep brown hair and clear blue eyes. It's not every day you see a blue-eyed Italian woman, you know. But pregnant and swollen, the idea that Paul could see me as anything other than your father's pregnant wife hadn't occurred to me. Both Paul and I were shocked when your father accused us of having an affair. He called me things I can't repeat. And he was ready to attack Paul, standing in the doorway, his eyes shooting fire. I must not have had enough to eat, I'd been so sick lately that I couldn't stomach food some days, I passed out. When I awoke, I knew what he thought. He looked down on me with disgust, left me there for a while, before he finally picked me up off the floor and led me to bed.

That night, after Paul packed his bags, just escaping the ridiculous fistfight your father threatened, I tried to talk to your father, but it was no use. He believed I had cheated. He told me I wasn't worth the effort it took to spit out words when I suggested we talk. He didn't want to upset me in my condition. Right! He told me to leave and sleep. It was all so confusing. I packed up several bags; I packed so, so slowly, hoping he would reconsider. I cried all the while, shaking and hardly there, and could not believe this man I love didn't understand me. It didn't help that I was pregnant, which seems to lure out the waterworks anyway. But this was too real, and life crippling, for me. I left your things, all the cute stuffed animals and onesies and the softest bath towels I had bought for you and stashed away for when I could create a nursery, give you a piece of our home, until the time your father was ready for me to come back.

I'm still waiting for your father to reconsider. I hope that he'll realize how wrong he was, then come to me penitent. I'll forgive him despite my own anger and feelings of betrayal because the life I imagined I would give you is one with all of us there. I must go now. My eyelids are heavy, and sleep calls. I wish your father would too.

Love always, Your dearest mother MonaLee

# Chapter Five

*"These your unusual weeds to each part of you
do give a life."*
-William Shakespeare

$\mathcal{P}$hil slammed his good hand down on the snooze button. The pillow over his head shielded his eyes from the intruding morning sun.

Five minutes later, when the beeping started up again, Phil flung the pillow to the floor where it landed on top of a pile of fallen, tin blinds from the window. Phil got up and groggily kicked through a pile of clothes.

The bathroom was piled with dirty towels. A puddle of soap lay stagnant on the counter. He was living in filth. Back home, there had always been someone hovering—someone ready to pick up his dirty towel and to straighten his bed sheets, do his laundry, and put his books in a neat pile on his nightstand. Now his little effort meant living in this mess. He would probably try harder if he were living there alone, but he wasn't willing to pick up his towels and those of the other guys too, which is what he'd have to do in order to get to some level of cleanliness. Phil picked a familiar looking towel from the pile, still a little damp, and smelled it. It would have to do. He'd need to get to the laundromat soon though. Just another thing to add to the list.

By eight, he and the rest of the guys were on their way to another day at the resort. Phil's arm, although still a bit sore after several weeks, was healing. He was finally able to remove the sling and wrap. Phil's name was scribbled on the day's schedule tacked on the lift-operator lodge wall next to Hellacious, the topmost lift at the resort.

After two weeks of being assigned to the lower lifts, he was finally making his way back to the real slopes. Piper's name, as always, was beside Snow Hare. She was assigned to the bunny slope every day. She'd get more exciting assignments if she'd only learn to ride. Phil had tried to teach her. He wouldn't waste any more time on her, someone who was clearly not interested in good advice.

Last week, she'd been standoffish. What Phil thought was exciting—*who wouldn't love a sled ride down the slope?*—and would certainly make her fall head over heels for him had pushed her away. Well, she had technically fallen with her head next to her heels when the board had landed beside the lift shack, but she didn't seem to find the humor or charm in their little adventure. He didn't understand why this bothered him so much, why her indifference made him care all the more. *Why did it seem a personal challenge now to get Piper to see him?* He felt himself lingering in the lodge just a little too long, hoping to see her face before he headed up the mountain.

He waited as long as he dared, but there was no Piper. He grabbed his board and made his way to Frozen Tempest, the lift that traveled up the mountain to get to the good steep trails. And there she was, already at Snow Hare, shoveling the ramp with that pom-pom bobbing on top of her hat.

One of the local lifties, a skier named Justin, was working Snow Hare with her. While Piper shoveled, he sat in the shack. Phil didn't know why he cared. He didn't care. He'd just keep walking. No, he needed that guy to know he should be helping. Yes, he'd go tell him so. Actually, now that he thought about it, Piper had done the shoveling for him while he nursed his arm back and hadn't seemed to mind doing it. The pot calling the kettle black. No, he couldn't say anything. He dropped his head and walked on with his snowboard tucked under his arm.

"Phil," a girl's voice shouted, from the snowboard rental shack. "Where were you last night?"

Phil looked up and saw Summer standing in the doorway of the snowboard repair shop, poised there with her arm resting vertically and her hair falling over her shoulder. Phil nodded his head up in that cocky attitude she seemed to like in him.

"Stop by for a sec, will ya?" she shouted, this time even louder.

Phil checked back to see if Piper had noticed but she was still dutifully shoveling snow.

Summer wrapped her arms around his neck and kissed him, full-on shoving her tongue in his mouth. He was holding his snowboard to the side still and he let her do it. Just a puppet, following the strings or whatever. It felt so staged, like some sort of show. He wondered who his audience was—and while he thought it might make Piper notice him a little, he didn't really want her to notice this.

"Dude, it's nine in the morning," Phil said, backing away.

"Why weren't you at the party last night? I waited around until midnight for you," she said, tucking his beanie over his ear where it had come up a bit. Sort of motherly, which didn't fit her style. Nah, it was possessively. Phil looked back up toward Snow Hare again and this time Piper was standing still leaning on the shovel, looking his way. He lifted his free hand to wave, but she turned away as he did, which made him feel like an awkward grade school boy. He looked back to Summer.

"So, what can possibly interest you there?" Her face had fallen and lost its cheery luster from before.

"What do you mean?"

"Why do you keep looking at her?"

Phil shook his head, buying time. He certainly didn't know how to respond to Summer about something he didn't quite understand himself.

"She's not your type," she said.

"She's a friend, all right? We worked the lift together when I was stuck down here." Then Phil raised his eyebrows, expecting her to follow up with exactly what his type was.

"She's just so—homely."

This was so unlike Summer, this jealousy. And Phil didn't like it. This wasn't part of their "arrangement." He didn't go following *her* around like she was his girlfriend or something. He let her do what she wanted, and he expected the same courtesy. Phil looked at her, shaking his head again and hoping she'd realize how ridiculous she sounded.

"I've gotta go." Phil turned and began clomping away through the snow in his boots.

"Don't embarrass me," Summer said, to his back.

Phil stopped in his snow tracks and thought for a second, then turned slowly back to face her. "Be careful, Summer." As he turned and resumed his trek across the snow toward the main lift, Phil consciously kept himself from looking over at Piper. He didn't want to know what she'd seen or heard.

*Don't embarrass me,* Phil thought back on Summer's last scornful words. She wouldn't have the chance to be embarrassed. He was through with her crap.

\*\*\*

The sky began dropping hard ice pellets onto Phil's face as the lift carried him up the mountain where he was to work the top shack. He zipped up his coat and nestled his face inside the fleece collar, then he pushed down his beanie as far as it would go and settled his goggles onto his face. The expanse of snow below stretched over the mountain like a thick, clean blanket making him wish he were back at home in bed with freshly laundered sheets. He closed his eyes and just felt the movement of the lift taking him up.

Phil didn't know why he felt so low. Coming here, taking this break, the snowboarding—it had all been his idea. But he felt an emptiness that he'd never had before, even last year when he'd been floundering in college. At least then he had moments and a purpose, even if it was just barely passing another class. He could look down and sometimes see a textbook in his hand. But here, always surrounded by his boarding buddies and their heaps of clothes and other crap, he felt restless. Maybe tonight he'd make dinner for the guys. He would make something good—maybe the soup he used to help his mother make when she was in the mood for cooking. He much preferred her homemade meals to the prepared stuff by the cook his mother had brought in several times a week. He loved her Italian dishes that were old family recipes she swore she'd never divulge, unless he helped her. He would sit at the kitchen island and chop things for her, potatoes, onions and red peppers, while she was stirring away at the stove with the smell of sausage filling the kitchen. He'd loved that soup and longed for it again. Yes, that's what he'd make tonight—his mother's Italian potato and sausage soup. Maybe he'd make up some homemade rolls too. He'd stop by the grocery store on his way home from work.

With that plan in place, Phil felt a little more purposeful. Just the thought of remembering those smells and that time spent as a sous chef for his mom brought a smile, still hidden underneath the folds of fleece in the inside of his coat.

***

S now dumped all morning. Few skiers and boarders were out, which was fine by Phil as he got to hang out in the Hellacious shack while it was a ghost town out there, just shoveling a little to keep the ramp smooth every once in a while. In his boredom, he looked around the unfinished, wooden walls of the shack while he sat on the stool. He began reading the markings scribbled all over, from years of bored lifties doodling their presence, leaving their marks. On the back wall, smack dab in the center was a mammoth drawing of a fatty with smoke curlicues swirling up to the ceiling. Maybe he should just give in and start smoking all the crap his friends were. They seemed to be having a much better time here than he was. Phil shook his head, smirked, and continued reading the wall to pass the time. Some girl named Jenny was in love with Luke. A dude with a black marker was quite fond of the word "ass" and decorated the walls with every ass-word he could think of: ass wipe, asshole, kiss ass. "JIMI HENDRIX RULES" was scribbled in a line, over and over and over, in the middle of the wall like wainscoting all around the entire shack. In the bottom corner, with tiny, neat pencil script, there was a faint single line sitting so inconspicuously—yet out of place—that Phil almost missed it: Love is a secret, snowflakes falling in the dark.

    He looked back to the chairs heading up the mountain and saw a couple skiers getting off the lift. He sat down at his chair in front of the big window and watched them shift down the ramp, all the while thinking about those words—*Love is a secret.* He said aloud the words and watched the snow fall silently outside. He thought about Piper, when they'd worked the Snow Hare lift together, and remembered the way the snowflakes landed so softly and dissolved into her mass of long, dark hair. And the way he felt when they spoke together, like he was the only person in the world. Her eyes, all round and blue, could only keep him in their view. All her attention was on him, and only him. *That wasn't what he wanted, was it?*

    Summer had given him what he thought he should want—sex with no strings attached, a warm body in his bed, a girl all the other guys wanted. That's what every guy wants. So when Phil saw Summer riding up the lift alone later that morning, he wasn't sure what exactly it meant. She balanced a Styrofoam container in her gloved hands while she rode her snowboard expertly down the ramp. Even Phil, despite his feelings from earlier, couldn't stay angry. He felt so lonely that Summer's small act of kindness would go a long way.

He watched from the open shack door as Summer set down the cup, removed the board from her boot, and set it to the side. She stomped through the heavy snow to him and held out the container with both hands, a pretty, pleading smile on her lips.

"I brought you some soup," she said, and Phil held the door open for her to enter. She stepped in and he took the container. "It's quite a storm out there. Frankie was making up some cheddar broccoli soup down in the kitchen, and I thought it'd warm you up."

"Thanks," he said, and meant it. She took off her gloves, shook off her beanie and errant snowflakes stuck in her hair, then leaned against the wall.

"I'm sorry, you know, about earlier." She brought a tentative hand toward his face and cupped his chin. It was cold.

Phil shook his head in lieu of a response.

She smiled and pulled two plastic spoons from her coat pocket, then held them before him with a bright smile on her face. "Wanna share?"

He nodded and took the lid off the Styrofoam container. Steam billowed out and he brought it close to his face. The smell of broccoli—not exactly Phil's favorite—filled the shack. Summer squeezed on the stool beside him and they both took turns with the creamy, warm lunch. The soup tasted good. Both Summer and this soup had managed to surprise him.

The soup warmed him up and by the time he swallowed his last spoonful, he had also warmed back up to Summer. Phil let her kiss him. A softer, more sincere kiss than the earlier one.

"What do you think of this?" he asked, pointing to the little gem of words on the wall. *Love is a secret, snowflakes falling in the dark.*

Summer cocked her head, read it aloud and said, "Hmmm. Sounds like a poem." She began to put her gloves and beanie back on. "If you're into that kind of thing."

"Of course I'm not," Phil said, thinking back on the book that had smitten Piper so much that she seemed to be more interested in words than in him.

Summer shook her head. "I didn't think so. Words have to do when you have nothing better in front of you." She kissed him again, an attempt to solidify their being "back on," Phil assumed.

After she left, he sat and thought. He tried to think about Summer, but his thoughts veered from the blond girl to the brown-haired one who was always slumped over a book. He tried to remember the few conversations he'd had with Piper. It wasn't the words they'd said, but there was something about Piper that Phil needed. He wasn't sure what it was but he knew he wouldn't be able to find it in Summer, no matter how long he looked. The snow let up just before his two o'clock lunch break, and the mountain was dazzling with the shimmery, sparkly layer of white. In a few hours, after the boarders and skiers plowed through, there would be tracks and divots and the sparkle would be gone.

The layer on top, Phil thought, was only temporary. There had to be something deeper. Phil realized, with clarity, that was it. There was something deeper inside Piper that shone out through those ice-blue eyes. A sparkle that something was alive, so alive, like poetry inside her. But he had to dig to find more or wait for the snow to melt.

Phil felt alive with something burning inside him. Words. This was crazy and so not him. He picked up the dull pencil wedged into the lift-shack checklist he'd need to fill out before he went on break. But first. But first, he had to add something. His secret.

He checked to make sure no one was coming up the lift and went to the corner where the poem sat waiting. He knelt down and painstakingly added to the words about love being a secret.

"*At light, I realize it has covered me,*
*swallowed me.*"

Phil stood up, satisfied, and smiled at his work. Maybe he had some words of his own inside him that would connect with Piper's. With that, he wedged the pencil back into the clipboard and picked up his shovel to shape the ramp before his lunch break, which he planned to spend riding. Leaving his own mark in the pure, untouched snow.

Later that night, Phil stood in the kitchen with the uncooked potatoes, sausage and onions on the counter before him with the scent of his mom's soup so ripe in his memory, while his friends sat in the living room watching something loud on the TV. He stood overwhelmed and reconsidered. His body was tired from a full day of work and the mountain of dirty dishes in the sink looked insurmountable. The scent of the kitchen was nothing close to the sweet sausage he wanted but of days-old, crusted marinara sauce mixed with a stagnant pool of brown water, part of a sandwich floated atop the pool. *Seriously, he thought, couldn't they at least throw the sandwich in the trash?*

Phil turned the tap on to get the hot water running and started moving around some of the dishes into orderly piles of plates and cups and silverware. He listened irritably to the laughing of the guys from the other room and with a pang, Phil realized he didn't own a pot large enough to hold soup. They only had one small pot that was just barely big enough for macaroni and cheese or SpaghettiOs. With that thought, he packed the food into the refrigerator and went to join his friends in the living room to rest a while. He had a can of chili and some boxed macaroni and cheese— maybe in a while, when he was less tired, he'd make up some chili mac.

## Chapter Six

*"I told you what would come of this: beseech you.*
*Of your own state take care: this dream of mine,*
*Being now awake, I'll queen it no inch farther,*
*But milk my ewes, and weep."*
*-William Shakespeare*

After a long day standing at the lift while penny-sized snowflakes fell around her, Piper grabbed her backpack and escaped into the darkening evening without so much as a goodbye to the other lifties. She hiked to her car in the employee parking lot, leaving tunnels each time she picked up her foot to take another step. When she finally reached her car, it looked like a fort built by children. She could see just the blue from the side mirrors of her car jutting out. She swept the snow from the door and fitted the key into the lock, then struggled to wrestle the ice-glued door open. Some snow fell in clumps as the door finally swung out. Piper started the engine to warm things up, threw her bag in the passenger seat and grabbed her snow brush from the back seat.

As she brushed loose snow from the windshield and the surrounding windows, Piper tried to ignore the shouting and laughing of the rest of the lifties as they hiked to their cars. She didn't look up, just ran images through her head of Phil as he'd stopped at her lift on his way down the mountain. She'd been manicuring the ramp into a sleek layer of hard snow so that she could finish everything from the "closing the lift" checklist. At the "Please Load Here" sign lying flat on the ground, she was indenting inside the letters with the pointy edge of the shovel to make sure the words were framed just right. Justin, who had been working the lift with her all day, had taken off early to ski a couple extra runs. That's when Phil showed up, like clockwork. She heard the scrape of his snowboard and felt a spray of powder shooting up from his sharp stop. When she turned around, Phil was standing before her still strapped into his snowboard.

"Hey, you," he'd said. "Miss me?"

Piper nodded her head tentatively and looked at him, waiting for him to take the lead. *Shouldn't you be with your girlfriend?* she thought, remembering the kiss she'd witnessed the other morning, but instead said, "You just can't keep away from Snow Hare, huh?"

"Something like that," he said, kneeling down to unstrap his snowboard. He wiped the snow from the front of his board, which exposed curling ocean waves, blue and foamy. He wrapped the board under his arm like he was carrying textbooks to class. "I'll walk you to the lodge."

Piper started walking with him but remained silent. She wasn't sure what to say to him. He made her nervous.

"Some storm, huh?" she came up with, finally.

"It hasn't let up all week," he said. "Not that I'm complaining. This is the reason we came here from California."

"California, huh?" Piper said. *Why did she keep saying, huh?* She felt a little stupid and then realized with a pang that, while he knew all about her and where she'd come from, she never thought to ask about him. Her mother would be mortified with her lack of social grace. Piper nodded over to Phil's board, which exposed several sharks circling. "That makes sense. Your board. You miss the ocean?"

"As much as I miss my mom," he said, hesitating. "A lot."

"I wouldn't have pegged you as a mama's boy," Piper said. "A surfer I can see, sure, but not a mama's boy."

"There's a lot you don't know about me," he'd said, and that's when Phil's friends had shown up floating by on their boards, all loud and obnoxious, which shut Piper up completely.

Hearing their rowdy voices again in the parking lot made her chest constrict as Piper continued her quest to remove snow from her car. Even after the windows were cleared, a good foot of snow was still packed on top of the roof. She got in the driver's seat, revved the engine, and lurched forward. She took it slow, maneuvering in and out of snow divots on the ground. Just when the street was in sight, her car was stuck in a big pit. She revved and revved, gassed it over and over, and she could feel her wheels spinning but the car wouldn't climb. She flung her head back, resisting the urge to beat the steering wheel in frustration. *Great. Now what?*

Piper sat in her car. On the radio, Elgar's Cello Concerto—one of her all-time favorites—began and she turned up the dial to listen to the familiar melody. She leaned her head back, closed her eyes, and tried to calm herself, just listening as the soothing music swept over her.

After a while, she took a deep breath, pulled her hat down a little more, and then climbed back out into the cold. She landed in at least two feet of snow and trudged her way toward the front tires that were packed in snow. She was discouraged but grabbed her snowbrush and scraper and began trying to scrape some of the hardened snow from her tire tracks. She was well into her task—even encouraged enough to convince herself this just might work—when the thumping of loud music came nearer and an SUV pulled beside her.

"You need help?" Phil's voice called out.

"Nope. I've got it all under control."

"I can't leave you here," he said, shaking his head.

"Go," she said, suddenly aware that the cello concerto was turned up as loud as his own punk music playing from his car. It embarrassed her that she was rocking out to a cello concerto.

"No can do," he said, shaking his head. "We'll push you out."

"No, really," she said. "You don't need to get out of your—" But the doors were opening and the guys were falling out. *How many of them were packed in there?*

"Okay, okay," Piper said. "Let me put the car in neutral." She felt relieved to get into the front seat so she could turn off the radio, which she did first, then shifted into neutral. She rolled down the window. "I'm ready."

There they all were, with their hands gripping her bumper, and Phil called out, "1-2-3," then they pushed and pushed and pushed so hard the car began climbing up the mound and then back down into another. She hadn't expected the big surge of movement and hadn't gripped the steering wheel tight enough. It wasn't until she started veering down a sharp decline to the right, by a load of pine trees that she tightened her grip and tried to pull the car back onto the parking lot, but now it was too late. She braked as hard as her foot would let her, but the car wouldn't stop and she was heading straight for a tree. She swerved and barely missed it, where it stopped with a thud into the even deeper snow. She looked up and all the guys were standing up on the parking lot looking down at her.

"Thanks," she said, lowly, to herself. "For all the help."

"Sorry about that," Phil yelled down. "I guess we didn't know our own strength."

Piper released a large sigh and wondered what she would do now. There was no way she was going to get her car out now. She stood looking at her car's plight. It was stuck until some of the snow could be cleared away.

"I can take you home," Phil said.

Piper nodded. She grabbed her bag and climbed up the snow bank where Phil was. All the other guys had left, waiting in the car. He leaned in toward her as she came near. "I'm sorry. That went horribly wrong. We were just trying to help."

"I know," Piper said.

"Let me drop off the guys, and I'll take you home."

Piper followed him to his SUV. He opened the passenger side door and said, "You mind, Heath?"

"Dude?"

Phil held the door open for him.

"I can sit back there—" Piper said and looked cautiously into the back seat filled with Phil's friends and her chest began to tighten again.

"No," Phil said. "Heath doesn't mind."

"Dude! I had shotgun!" Heath said. Then he smiled at Piper, patted his thighs. "You can sit on my lap."

"Go. Now," Phil said, motioning to the back door.

Piper looked down at her boots as he fell out of the door laughing and piled into the back seat, now really squished together. The seat was still warm where Heath had been sitting and she felt strange, being here in this car, in Heath's spot, completely unwanted. Well, by most of them anyway. Phil seemed to want her there, which baffled her.

"I'm sorry to take your seat—" Piper said, into the rearview mirror. The music was playing so loud she knew he couldn't hear her, but Phil did.

"No need to apologize," Phil said. "Heath's glad to offer his seat."

Piper sat silent the rest of the ride to Phil's apartment. The beat of the loud music dictated the rate her heart was beating. She listened in as the guys spoke of some "gnarly mammoth cliff" they jumped in the backcountry. When they pulled into the parking lot of a cluster of buildings, all the guys tumbled out. Piper stayed in the front seat. Phil lured her out by promising it would only be a minute so he could change his clothes.

She followed him into the cluttered, and smelly, apartment and stood near the front door.

"I'll be right back. Make yourself at home. Have a snack," Phil said and gestured toward the kitchen, then disappeared around a corner.

She stood there alone, listening to the guys in the living room still discussing Heath's "biff" from the cliff and her cold hands started to shake. *Why did these guys make her so uneasy?* She had no business in this apartment and wished she had something to do with her hands. She noticed the mound of dishes in the sink. As much as she didn't want to seem servantile—a girl among all these guys—even more, she didn't want to be in the room with them. And the thought of her cold hands submerged in hot, soapy water sent delicious shivers up her spine. So she shed her coat, rolled up her sleeves, turned the faucet on hot, and began separating the dishes on the counter to clear out the sink. Under the counter, she found a small, unopened bottle of dishwashing soap and filled the sink until it was overflowing with suds. She stood there, her back to the continued loud conversation, soaking and washing and scrubbing and rinsing. She was well into her chore when Phil returned.

"You're doing our dishes?"

She shrugged. "Sorry."

"You're apologizing? Would you like to move in?" he asked, with a smile that let her glimpse the little boy he once was, much less a threat.

Piper looked around and took a sniff of the lingering smell of rotten food.

"No thanks."

"I hate to stop what you're doing, but... ready to go?"

Piper reached under the sink where she found the dishwashing soap and handed Phil a crumpled but clean towel. "You can dry."

Piper handed Phil dishes, and he dutifully dried and put them away in the sparse cupboards. There was light talk, at first about spoons and spooning. When Phil held up a fork, Piper stopped him. "That's enough on that line of conversation."

"Why are you helping me?" he'd asked her, serious now.

"You're helping me," she said. Phil was quiet as the music of shifting water and clanking dishes against the sink filled the silence. He smiled when she handed him the small pot from the chili mac last night, the last dish needing to be washed.

"Got pot?" Phil said, then grimaced. Piper rolled her eyes at his cliché and sorry attempt at humor.

"Pot's not really my thing," she said, pulling the drain from the sink and watching the water swirl down.

"Sorry," Phil said. "Bad joke. But seriously, do you have a soup pot at your apartment?"

Piper nodded.

"What if I make you dinner tonight—at your place? Soup. It's my mom's special recipe."

"It's a long way to drive to my apartment. And it's still snowing out there," she said, looking out the window.

"I bought all the ingredients yesterday, and this is the only pot I've got," Phil said, holding up the rusty old thing with a loose handle he'd just finished drying. "You'd be helping me out."

"I guess this favor thing is infectious," Piper said, smiling. He was kind of growing on her.

***

*A*s Piper sat in the car next to Phil, she held her hands in her lap and noticed them grasping each other like scared children. Phil's music was still beating its rapid pulse but was softer now. It was a nice offer, she knew, for him to drive her all the way home and then have to turn around and drive back. She had the hot chocolate guy's phone number still stored away, from when they'd studied together in that math group last month. She'd call him early tomorrow morning for a ride up the mountain, back to work.

It was getting late, and Piper was hungry. The ingredients for the soup were in the back seat. It was much less intimidating to have food sitting back there than Phil's friends. Phil was focused on the snow-packed road, his brow furrowed in concentration. He looked sweet, with his hands gripping the wheel, to keep the car steady, to keep her safe.

"So what kind of soup are we making?"

"I'll surprise you. You like sausage?"

Piper nodded. The thought of Phil in her little apartment made her nervous. She didn't regularly have visitors; in fact, had she ever even had one? If there was a study group, they met at the library. Her place was small, so small—just the one big room where she had her bed and dining and living area all overlooking each other and the tiny, pocket kitchen and her narrow bathroom. But at least it was tidy.

***

*P*hil toted the ingredients in a crinkling, plastic supermarket bag through the apartment door. The cats swarmed around Piper's legs like starving koi fish. They meowed and padded into the kitchen to the empty bowls.

"Okay, you two," she said, nudging them with her boot. "Step aside or you don't eat."

Phil followed Piper into the kitchen. He set the bag on the small counter and began unloading as Piper filled the cats' dishes.

"Help yourself," she said, to Phil. "The soup pot should be down there and the cutting board too." She gestured to one of the lower drawers. Since there wasn't much storage in the tiny kitchen, Phil didn't have to search long.

He began cutting up onions and red peppers and frying the sausage. The cats rubbed up against his ankles and looked up at him with wide eyes, eager to lavish their affections on a stranger for the mere thought of a dropped hint of meat.

"Are you sure you don't need me to help with anything?" Piper called in from the other room, where she was rifling through her mail at the small dining table.

"No," he said. "This is on me. Plus, how can I keep my mother's recipe secret with you hovering?"

Piper dropped her head back over the electric bill. "It smells good."

It was quite some time later when Phil finally brought over two filled bowls of the soup to where Piper sat studying at the table. He placed one before her and then settled opposite her on the other chair.

She brought a filled spoon to her mouth. On her tongue, the spicy but sweet and creamy flavors complemented each other. She looked across the table to him. He was still hot, but that wasn't what she saw anymore. She saw the face of someone who seemed to care about her. She didn't mind having him at her place, and it wasn't awkward as she'd feared. It was comfortable.

"I can see why you love this. It's good, really good," she said, taking another spoonful. One of the cats lay down on the rug by her feet.

"I haven't eaten anything decent in weeks," Phil said. He looked up at the stained-glass light hanging over the table. "So why'd you do it this way? Why didn't you live in the dorms and do the whole college thing?"

"I am doing the college thing, just not the way most do. It's cheaper here and it's easier to focus on school," she said. "Don't you miss it?"

"College? Nah. There'll be time for that later."

Piper nodded. "What do you want to do, though? What was your major?" There was so much to learn about someone from the answer to that question. If not a major that explained what they wanted to be or dreamed of being, then it was why they were choosing that course instead of what they truly wanted.

"Business."

"Hmmm. Really? You want to get into business. That's sensible."

"It's sensible and practical and all wrong for me. It's my father. I need an MBA, and then he said we can talk."

"About?"

"Getting me on at his company, training to take it all over, to being the big guy in charge someday."

"Sometimes we've got to be sensible," Piper said. "But what would you do if there were no expectations?"

"Besides snowboard the rest of my life?"

"Yeah, besides that." He put a spoonful of soup in his mouth as if he were buying himself a little more time, then he nodded. "Hike all the mountains in the world. But if you're going for something more traditional, I really don't know."

***

*H*is answer was reassuring. She didn't know, either, what she wanted in life. For now, it was okay to just meander along.

When they finished dinner, they began clearing the table. She looked up at the clock on the wall. It was almost ten o'clock already, much later than she usually ate. She'd gotten off to a late start. She filled the sink and began scrubbing the dishes. While her sudsy hands wiped down the frying pan, she felt it like a sock in the stomach that she was without her car. She was helpless without it. Phil brought over the last of the bowls. It was sweet, really, the way he was doing little things, trying to be helpful. Like they were playing house or something.

"Need me to dry?" he asked.

"You cooked, I'll clean up," Piper said. "Why don't you go have a seat and take a load off for a little while? I'll be done in a minute."

He nodded and strolled off in the direction of the small couch in front of an old fireplace. A platform of candles was nestled inside the hearth. Beside the mantel were bookshelves built into a doorframe that had been walled in, to make the main floor two separate apartments. Piper kept scrubbing and watched him sit down on the couch.

He was looking up into her bookshelf. "That's a lot of books."

"Yep," she said, smiling to herself remembering their first encounter when she told him he'd have to read *Jane Eyre* if he ever wanted to see her ride a snowboard again.

He stood, plucked a book from the shelf, and sat back down. "Why do you have candles in your fireplace?"

"I never light a fire. I light the candles instead."

"Why?"

"No wood," she shrugged, placing the final bowl on the towel to dry.

She sat beside him and looked at the book in his lap. *Jane Eyre.* Maybe he was going to take her up on that offer after all.

"What if I went out and rounded some wood up?"

"If you think you can. It is a working fireplace."

"I'll see what I can find," he said. He put on his boots and disappeared out the back door. Piper went to the window and watched him inspecting some snow-covered twigs near the edge of the parking lot, where several trees stood bare and shivering. Piper changed into a comfortable pair of jeans and a fitted t-shirt by the time Phil came back in, nudging his boots off before stepping back into her apartment, carrying a roped bundle of firewood.

"Wow, you just chopped down a tree?" Piper asked.

"You can buy firewood around the corner at the Quick Mart," he said. He knelt down by the hearth and began stacking the wood in a teepee shape. "Got any newspaper?"

Piper shook her head. "I have a couple old phone books, though." He nodded and she went to the closet and pulled out a thick, yellow book. She knelt beside him with the book. They yanked out fistfuls of pages, crumpling and nudging them into the hollows between the wood. Dorcas lay down beside Phil and batted at a crumpled ball of paper. When their work was nearly complete, Piper brought a box of matches from the kitchen.

It was getting late and Phil should probably head home, but as Piper and Phil sat on the couch before the crackling fire, peace came over her and she could feel the warmth of Phil's leg against her knee as she sat cross-legged. She didn't want him to leave. He was reading the second chapter of Jane Eyre while Piper held her accounting textbook in her lap. The fire cast a glow over his face as he sat hunched over the book.

"Why me?" she whispered. Her voice shook. "What's in this for you?"

He looked up from the book and closed it. "Nothing."

Piper put her book on the floor next to where Mopsa was sleeping by the fire.

"You should go," Piper said, even though all she wanted was him in her arms.

"I know," he whispered. "I just don't want to." They stared into the fire and he said, "I want to know something about you that nobody else knows."

"Nobody?"

"Nobody."

The apartment was silent but for the crackling fire as Piper thought. She smiled and said, "I secretly love—" She paused for dramatic effect and finished her sentence, "liver and onions." She laughed and placed her arm on his shoulder. He laughed too. She knew she should remove her hand, but she couldn't will it back, like it was magnetized to him. "It was an old, family meal my mom used to make. I told her I hated it and would sit at the table and screw around, but I kind of liked it. I miss my mom's liver and onions."

"What about you? One secret no one else knows." She left the hand on his shoulder, so lightly, like a wind-blown leaf that should have been long gone for the winter but was left behind.

"I guess I shouldn't have started this," he said, settling deeper into the couch cushions. Another long pause. He turned slowly and said, "I don't want to take over my father's company. Not now, not ever." He swallowed, so hard that Piper could hear him forcing down unwanted tears.

"Why don't you tell him?"

"Because I've always been expected to do this, to take it over. It's always been in the books, like a map of my life already written before I was in kindergarten. Everyone expects me to do it, but I don't want to do it. What if I fail? What if I just don't have what it takes?"

Piper gently squeezed his shoulder and let the silence hang in the air a little longer.

"Is this why you're here? Taking your sabbatical? To buy more time?"

He nodded and didn't meet her eyes.

"Okay," she said, still conscious of her hand on him. "I'll tell you a secret better than liver and onions. Maybe this will make you feel better. As a child, I wanted to be a musician. And everyone expected me to be something special—from the time I first showed promise as a child playing the viola. And I've failed, already. I don't have what it takes." Piper didn't expect the words, the honesty, to come shooting out of her, like sparks from the fire. She pulled her hand away from him now, and tried to hold back tears, hold back the pain she'd tried to recover from since the audition last year. "So there, I win."

Phil turned to her and wrapped his arm tentatively around her shoulder, brought her to him. They were chest to chest and she melted into him.

"How can you have failed already? You're young. You still have lots of time."

She shook her head against his shoulder. "I didn't get in to the university orchestra. I needed that scholarship. So I switched my major. I didn't know how elitist everything would be in the music department. I just loved music. I didn't think it would make or break me if I didn't hold my bow just the right way or if my bowings weren't exactly what they thought it should be. Where's the artistic expression in that? I just let myself be guided by the music. They didn't want me, they didn't see anything there, so I quit playing."

"Completely?"

Piper nodded.

"You haven't played since?"

Here Piper hesitated and her eyes were drawn to the leather, viola case resting where she left it in the corner, just a little abandoned. "Well, my mom just sent me a new viola. For my birthday last week. And, okay, so I have picked it up a couple of times just recently."

"Play for me," he said.

She shook her head against his chest. "No," she whispered.

"I don't care how you hold your bow." He looked deep into her eyes. "I want to know what it was that shaped you."

"I can't. Plus, there's a noise ordinance here. No music after ten." She shrugged, playfully. "Still, you wouldn't understand. It's not your type of music."

"Fine. Can I try to play it?" He struggled to get up.

"Wait, no, you can't," she said, hopping off the couch to stop him.

"Piper, one of us is going to play that violin."

She shook her head. "It's like a violin, but no, it's a viola."

"Like I said, one of us is going to play it—either you or me. I'll let you pick."

She stood reluctantly and drew the case from its quiet corner. As she sat beside Phil on the couch, she opened the case.

"It's ridiculous, really," she said. "This is an old, old viola. I don't know how my parents could afford it. And the tone is amazing. But I just can't let you touch it. What if you break a string I can't afford to have fixed?"

She pulled the viola from the velvet, along with the bow. Then she stood near the couch and said, "Just something soft and simple so it doesn't wake up the whole apartment house. It's called *Vocalise*."

Piper closed her eyes and pulled a thread of quivering, crying notes from the viola. She moved slowly, like she was mourning a loss or loving a small child. It didn't last long, only minutes. Then she pulled the instrument from position and it hung from her hand along her leg. Phil stood and came near with a look in his eyes—

one part sad, one part mesmerized. He wrapped his arm around her and put his hand on the back of her head, pulling her to him, then kissed her slow and sad, like the melody that had rung out so softly moments before. And she kissed him back with the same slow and soft feeling she'd just played, the melody still streaming from somewhere deep inside her.

## Chapter Seven

*"This is the prettiest low-born lass that ever
Ran on the green sward: nothing she does or seems
But smacks of something greater than herself,
Too noble for this place."*
-William Shakespeare

The kiss was an epiphany. He didn't want it to stop. Ever. She grabbed for him, hungrily, made him feel needed, wanted. And he liked that feeling. Especially from Piper, who was usually so reserved. Her viola knocked against his knee as she still held onto it.

She pulled away, held her finger up to signal just-a-moment, and walked backward away from him, but not pulling her eyes away from his. She set the viola carefully into the case and then rushed back to him, like she was afraid he wouldn't still be here, stepping back into the kiss.

He hadn't made a conscious decision to kiss her, but it just seemed to fit the moment. And she was kind of at fault really—her music had pulled him to her, like a magic spell. Here in this place, just a room really, with the warmth from the fire crackling nearby, it was the perfect moment. A soft spot in his crazy, messy world. This girl was so unlike any he had ever looked twice at. And maybe that had been his problem all this time. Maybe he was looking in the wrong places.

When the kiss came to an end, she looked to him, as if uncertain whether to ask him to leave or kiss him again. He hoped the words wouldn't come that would send him out into the cold night alone. Thankfully, she went to the back door to lock it and slid onto the couch beside him, where they kissed some more.

It's not like he didn't want to sleep with her, he did. In fact, he *really* did. *Wasn't that the natural step?* They were kissing. She liked it, he could tell. But no, he couldn't do this. He had to will his hands not to go to questionable, questionable to her, that is, territory. He wanted her to trust him. And although it seemed natural to sleep with her, he wouldn't try.

Piper seemed so innocent. *Wouldn't it just complicate things if they started off going too far?* Not now, not yet. She was like a stray dog that had finally succumbed and was sniffing his hand. He wouldn't scare her off with any sudden movements. So he settled in beside her, stroked her hair and her arm, and then let himself drift off to sleep after she stilled.

It must have been hours into the morning when he was awakened by her whimpering. It was a low cry mixed with unintelligible words. She was kicking, restless, and crying out. Phil held her more tightly, and she burrowed into him. Her breathing changed; he could tell she was awake.

"Are you all right?" he whispered into her ear.

She nodded. "I woke you, didn't I?" she asked. "I have nightmares. There's this woman who comes to me in my dreams. Sounds crazy, I know. I'm sorry I woke you."

"No worries," he said, and she clung to him like he was protection from her dreams. He held her tighter. Yes, he would protect her. Maybe it was the stillness of the night or her breath on his neck or the calm he felt at this moment, but all he wanted to do was to be her protector.

\*\*\*

He awoke the next morning before the sun. The fire had died to glowing embers and a cushy blanket was halfway over them. The orange cat lay against his leg. Piper was still sleeping, breathing a steady rhythm, and he tried not to move. He didn't want to wake her. The cat must have sensed he was awake as it stood and stretched, and then stepped onto his chest, circled a couple times, and settled down again. That did it; Piper was awake.

"Morning, bright eyes," he said, pushing her hair from her face.

Piper broke into a sleepy smile. "Good morning," she said.

They chatted for a little while, then climbed from the couch after Piper's alarm clock began to go off, stretching and adjusting. Phil went off to use the bathroom. When he returned, Piper was sitting at the table with a carton of orange juice and a couple glasses, looking through a stack of papers. A small Christmas tree was lit in the corner.

"It's so strange," she mumbled to herself but what seemed to him as well. "I've read through all of them, but these letters seem so—unfinished. And I know I shouldn't be reading them."

"Why not?"

"They're not to me," she said, setting them down and pouring a glass of orange juice for him.

He sat down and picked up the top letter, "'Dear Perdita.' That's a strange name."

"I think it's pronounced—Purr-dee-ta. But you're right, it's not a name you hear every day. I found these letters in my viola case, just stuffed in the outside pocket," she started to explain. "It was a new—well, new to me, but used viola. Clearly, it's very old. Although I can't imagine the owner not noticing the bulging side pocket. There are hundreds of them. And all arranged from the beginning, like a novel to devour. Only it has a cliffhanger ending, and it's driving me crazy! Still, I feel like a voyeur reading them at all."

Phil shrugged matter-of-factly. "If you're worried, why don't you just ask the person you bought it from? Maybe they'd want them back."

"The viola was a birthday gift from my parents," she said. "I mentioned the letters to my mother, and she brushed me off, acting like it wasn't possible to contact the seller. They probably bought it from a violin shop. Maybe it had been there for years. She said not to worry about the letters, but I feel guilty. Having them, and reading them."

"Then just don't read them," Phil said.

Piper wrinkled up her nose. "I can't help it. They're calling to me. I think Perdita was stolen from her mother as a baby. It's really sort of a journal, which makes it seem even more like I'm invading her privacy."

"Can I read one?" Phil asked, sitting in the opposite chair.

"No, they're not to you!"

"They're not to you either."

"Okay," she said. "Good point. Just the first one. I'll get you some breakfast while you read. Do you want raisin bran or oatmeal?"

*\*\*\**

*P*iper asked Phil to drop her off at work before heading back for his buddies since it was on the way. Phil's apartment was just on the other side of the resort, in old town Park City along Main Street. None of his roommates had a car. They relied on Phil for rides to work. When he opened the front door to his apartment, Heath shouted out, "Come on. Let's go."

"Sorry, dude," Phil said. "I didn't mean to leave you hanging. If we leave now, we'll make it on time."

"So, what's gotten in to you?" Heath asked, before the others arrived. He was irritated, Phil could tell. "Seriously. This isn't like you."

"To spend the night with a girl? Where have you been?"

"Yeah, but that girl?"

"She needed a ride back to work this morning."

"You should have called. Dude, bros before hoes."

"She's not a hoe," Phil said, about as nicely as he possibly could considering the fact he wanted to punch Heath in the face. He looked right into him but managed to keep his balled fist inside his coat pocket.

"Speaking of hoes," Zane broke in as he and Tommy came to the door, pulling on their coats. "Summer came by last night, wondering where you were."

"Did you tell her?"

"Yeah," Zane said. "Ya got some explaining ta do."

"Come on," Phil said. "We've got to get to work."

As they drove up to the resort, Phil saw Piper's car still stuck near the fir trees on the edge of the lot. He selfishly hoped the sun wouldn't melt too much snow today and that Piper would be at his mercy again. He wanted to be with her again tonight, tomorrow, every night. He'd love to break his back sleeping on her sofa in that tiny apartment, with cats climbing around him.

He was assigned to work the top lift where he'd scribbled onto that poem. At noon, he sat down and breathed a sigh of relief that he hadn't been confronted by Summer all morning. Maybe she'd back off now that she knew he was kind of into Piper now; maybe he wouldn't have to explain. Summer didn't back down usually though. He knew that much.

Maybe Heath was right. He wasn't being himself. He sure as hell didn't feel like the Phil from before. It was as if he metamorphosed into a lovesick guy who could think of nothing more than the blue-eyed girl who enchanted him with her magical violin—no, it wasn't a violin. Viola.

He turned back and saw his unfinished poem fixed to the wall, waiting. He peered down the long lift. No one was coming. He already knew what he would write next. Underneath the poem's dangling unfinished tail, he added:

*"Am I still there when the storm's passed, after the thaw?"*

He didn't know if he'd be the same person after Piper. He kind of hoped not.

# Chapter Eight

*"The child was prisoner to the womb, and is*
*By law and process of great nature thence*
*Freed and enfranchis'd,"*
  -William Shakespeare

October 2, 1981

My dearest Perdita,

**H**e called. I'd been willing it, watching the phone and begging it to ring, and then the melodious ring came through! He asked my friend Paulina—who let me stay at her place—if he could talk to me. So that's it, I'm going home! He acted like he couldn't find me. Ha! He knew. How could he not know? I'm so happy that your father has realized his mistake and stopped the tragedy this could have been. He's sending a cab over to take me home. I'm taking a quick break from packing my meager things to write you now. You've become a journal to me, really, for now, until I can hold you in my arms. Then I'll say everything into your soft, tiny ear.

Your father said I could finally create that nursery for you. I'll do a bird theme, with musical notes. Don't you think that'd be just perfect for the sweet baby girl of a singer? Happy, little bluebirds belting their hearts out into the morning breeze. You're going to love it. Worms and flowers and fish hooks. And birds and cracked eggs in nests.

    I can't wait to fall into your father's arms. I'll forgive him. I will, completely. I won't hold a grudge. This is for you, all for you. I'll love him just like before so that we can be a family again. Me and him, and You. Beautiful, little you.

    I'm going to make everything so perfect for you. We'll be the perfect family, I'll be the perfect mother, apron and burp rag, and you'll dream away your nights in the perfect nursery. You're going to love this world created just for you. This free open place full of beauty and love.

    I must go now. The cab will be here soon.

    As will you. Mom

# Chapter Nine

*"What's gone, and what's past help,*
*Should be past grief."*
-William Shakespeare

October 5, 1981

My Perdita,

He never released his anger. When I first saw him back home, I went to him and wrapped him in my arms to show forgiveness for accusing me of cheating. He stood there, arms down like a statue, then he extricated himself from me as if I were disease-riddled. Acted like I needed sleep. He asked me to lie down, offered me a drink. I told him nothing alcoholic, please, then gestured to my ripe belly. But whatever he gave me cannot have been good for you; in fact, I'm sure it wasn't. I've been sick, very sick, vomiting so much. I think he's poisoned me.

  A doctor has been coming in to check on me. I've begged your father to take me to the hospital, but he insists his private doctor will be best. That way, my hospitalization wouldn't send out the "media pariahs." He's always called them that, yet gives them his most adoring smiles, his patient answers and gestures. Like a man dependent on public votes will. Pariah. Sarai. Foccacia.

I can't eat anything. It's been four days, and I worry I'm starving you. But I'm afraid of anything from his hand.

I beg the doctor to check your heartbeat every time he walks through the door. I'm not even sure where I am. I've certainly never been in this room of your father's estate. And your father is barely been here at all. I've asked for him, but everyone keeps telling me that he's busy or away.

Why would he want to hurt you? Why hurt me? I've given everything to him. All of me.

It was unusual for someone like him to take interest in me. What would a politician have in common with a rock singer? I've had one single, one really big single, and I had a nice following. I've opened concerts for some huge names, huge. And the audience puts up with my new or lesser known songs, then cheers and screams for "Let's Play in Love," my smash hit. It all happened so fast, my fame and popularity. One minute I was playing my guitar on a busy street in New York, begging for spare change in my open guitar case, and the next, I was hoisted on stage, my song playing in taxi cabs all through the city. It was exhilarating and wonderful. I went from homeless and sleeping on the spare couch of anyone who would have me to bringing in checks with more zeros than I knew were possible. The world couldn't get enough of me. Enough.

I'm not sure how I caught your father's eye. He is followed by a much different spotlight. His is political and pretentious; mine was colored with happenchance, hippy chic. But after we were both in the studio of the television station—he was a guest for a political news program and I was there for a musical spotlight of a talk show (of course they wanted me to sing "Let's Play in Love")—he sought me out and asked me to dinner afterward. I agreed, unsure what he would have to say to the likes of me, a high school dropout, so filled to the brim with music that I had no room in my head for geometry or history. But it felt right, pure conversational magic, not to mention the kiss before we parted. Bang! Pop!

Your father is important. Some even say he will be President of our country some day. I still don't know what he saw in me. He said my music swayed him; it didn't hurt that I was so different from the kind of woman he saw all day long. That's what he liked about me, he said, that I was cute and silly and fun. Not playing a part. Not afraid of anyone or anything.

Except now I am. And it's him I'm afraid of—and this place. Before, I had the run of the house. I was in charge of the house staff, but now the tables are turned. If I say I want something, they act like I'm a petulant child. I swear I've heard them snicker on occasion. Maybe I'm paranoid. I wish I had someone I trust to ask for help. Pajamas every day. I feel so cut off from the world. *Where's my agent when I really need her?* I wish I hadn't pushed away the guys from the band when I married. When I was pregnant, I blew them off like breath on a flickering match.

I asked for a walk moments ago. They say it's not good for me right now. I have to stay in bed, get better. Stay in loose-fitting clothes. Pajamas every day. For you. Then I think, yes, of course, for you.

I'm supposed to sleep now. Sleep will make me feel better. I am tired. I'll rest. But I feel restless in my dreams.

*Soon you'll be here. Soon. I need someone on my side, and I will always be faithfully yours,*
   *Mom*

## Chapter Ten

*"Tell me what blessings I have here alive,*
*That I should fear to die?"*
*-William Shakespeare*

November 30, 1981

My sweet angel Perdita,

**Y**ou were all I had. You were my only bright spot. Venus in a dark sky. I would have done anything for you. Anything. And now there's weightlessness in my arms where there should be you. I don't understand how one minute can mean the difference between holding your warm, breathing body and having nothing. How could you have left me? In this nothing world where babies die and moms are left empty-armed? My arms ache to hold you. My milk is dripping through my silk nightgown, searching for your breathing lips. I'm in pain, but no pain is worse than the thought of no you.

    I want to be gone from this horrible world. I want to be with you, wherever that is. I would follow you anywhere. All I have is this bed and these walls, and sterile, cold hands and faces that glide in and out of my room all day.

    I don't care where I am as long as you're in my arms. I will rock you to sleep, wherever you are.

    I am coming to you soon. Wait for me,
    Your mamma

# Chapter Eleven

*"The pale moon shines by night:
And when I wander here and there,
I then do most go right."*
—*William Shakespeare*

𝒫iper was right. You couldn't stop reading after the first letter. Thank goodness he ended up at her apartment again after work, as he couldn't get that first haunting letter out of his mind. And she'd told him to go ahead when he asked if she'd mind if he read a couple more.

Phil had been hoping for another chance to be with her and was shocked to see Piper standing before him as he gathered his things from his locker in the lifty lodge earlier. She asked him, as bold as love, if he'd take her home. He had been prepared to suggest it. He had been trying to come up with scenarios to present to Piper that wouldn't sound pathetic to be with her again. He was going to blame the snow that hadn't ceased falling all day on why he'd need to drive her back. But in Piper, there hadn't been any of that insecurity in her eyes that he'd seen before. And there hadn't been any reason for Phil to come up with an excuse.

"This will be the last time, I promise," she said. "I called my dad and he's arranging to have a truck tow my car out, but they were booked solid today."

"It's the most snow they've seen here for like fifty years," Phil said.

"The truck can be here tomorrow," Piper had said and that was how he'd ended up there, back in Piper's apartment. She'd need that ride back to the resort in the morning. It was an unspoken between them, that he'd be spending another night with her. He'd sleep with her in his arms.

Phil leafed through the stack of remaining letters. It was sad, really. The baby would have been close to his age.

"I guess she doesn't kill herself."

Piper looked up from her textbook and shook her head. "It gets worse."

"Worse than killing yourself?"

She nodded, then dropped her gaze back down to her textbook reading. Phil watched her loose curls fall over her shoulder and fought the desire to reach his fingers to touch her glossy, dark hair.

For dinner, they'd warmed up the leftover soup from the previous night. If he were back at his apartment, he'd be sitting in front of the television watching another snowboarding video with the guys or leaving for another smoke-filled party. Sitting in Piper's quiet apartment was a departure, but he liked it.

Phil wanted to get closer to Piper. He watched as she scribbled notes from her reading. She was so much prettier than he'd thought at first—that perfect little nose, those amazing, round blue eyes, lips shaped like the next kiss he couldn't wait for. He didn't want to interrupt her studying, but he stretched his foot under the table and rested it on hers. She looked up, smiled.

"You're bored," she said. Then she scrunched up her nose in a way that seemed so childish when he first met her but was now endearing and sexy.

"I was thinking of building another fire."

She shook her head. "We don't have any firewood left, and I don't want you to spend any more of your money."

"Why not?"

She shrugged. "You're already doing so much for me. You don't need to heat my apartment, too."

He set down the pile of letters onto the table and shuffled them.

"Well, we could just have a bonfire."

Her eyes went wide. "No way. I need those. Someone needs those."

"It would take care of your guilt. Then you wouldn't read them *again*."

"But I want to return them. It sounds like Perdita might be out there somewhere. Who knows? Maybe MonaLee's found her already."

"I have an idea," he said, tapping his fingers impatiently on the table.

"To find Perdita?"

"No," he said, then shrugged. "Although, we could probably find her if you really want to return the letters. It sounds like her mother used to be some kind of a big deal. I'm sure there'd be something out there about her." He stood, sliding the chair back. "Let's go earn some money for our firewood."

"What do you have in mind?" she asked, placing a sheet of paper into her textbook before closing its covers.

"It's a surprise," he said, grabbing her hand. "But bring your viola."

"No, no, no," she said, backtracking. "Okay, you can pay for the firewood."

He pressed his nose against hers, looking straight into her eyes. "This will be fun. I've always found street musicians intriguing."

"I can't," she said, reaching her arms around him, trying to keep him in one place, a mini wrestling match. "You don't understand."

He stopped trying to move and tilted her chin up to him. "Piper," he said. "Your playing is amazing."

She stood firm, shaking her head, nearly in tears.

"Okay," he said. "I just wanted to have some fun. That's all."

She kept her arms wrapped around him, which he didn't mind, and he leaned down and kissed her. She kissed him back, hesitantly at first, and then not hesitantly at all.

"I guess we could just stay in and do this all night," Phil said, when she pulled away.

Piper smiled, kissed him again quickly on the lips. "I wish I could, but homework calls."

"It's still calling?"

"Afraid so," she said, and seated herself before her textbook again. "Not that I'm the ethics police or anything, but if you don't mind invading some stranger's private correspondence, I guess you could keep reading." She gestured toward the letters. "You won't regret it."

## Chapter Twelve

*"Go on, go on:*
*Thou canst not speak too much, I have deserved*
*All tongues to talk their bitterest."*
*-William Shakespeare*

December 24, 1981

My Beautiful Perdita,

It's Christmas Eve, and I'm still hanging on. I'd been asking for your father, and he finally came, although I'm still not sure whether he was really here. It was dark, and I awoke when he crept into my silent room. Only the moon glistening through the smallest slit of window showed his face to me. This time, he wasn't all business. His face mirrored my own grief.

    He's been absent lately, staying away as if grief were contagious, or as if you didn't belong to him too. Tonight he knelt beside my bed and spoke to me. At first, I feigned sleep for fear that he would leave if he knew I was awake. I made my breaths regular and listened.

    He told me that he still loved me and that he loved you but was worried he'd made a mistake. I wanted to answer him, tell him I was in pain too and needed him by my side, but I didn't. I remained silent. He continued to himself but also to my sleeping form and said that jealousy—the thought of me with Paul—tore him apart and this felt like the only thing he had control of. He begged my forgiveness as his tears soaked the sheets of my bed. He begged for me to understand that even now he couldn't make things right. He couldn't have the media lurking around, meddling in his private business, broadcasting it to the world. He would keep me here, under his thumb. I wanted to tell him I would forgive him for leaving me all alone in this, making me suffer the grief as if alone on an island. As if he heard my thoughts through the silence, he answered that he felt it too. That the grief of losing the baby girl tore him to pieces. He wanted my forgiveness again. He gripped my arm—I swear it's bruised today—and implored me to forgive what he'd done. That he wished he could go back and do things again, but it was too late. Much too late. Shivering cold. The shaking wouldn't stop.

    He promised me he would take care of you. I don't understand what he meant; maybe he *was* sleep-talking because he can't take care of you where you are now. *How could he?* Maybe he has felt grief more than I knew. Maybe he's just been really good at hiding it. Maybe he's so upset he can't see the reality of your death.

    I couldn't control myself any longer. I wanted him near me, so I let my hand cross the barrier to touch him, and I pulled him up to me on the bed. He curled himself around me and cried. I cried along with him, my body wouldn't still for the longest hour. And our tears pooled together and washed us along the tide to sleep.

    The next morning, he was gone. No trace of him, no indentation in the bed where his body had been beside me, no dampness on the sheets where his tears had fallen. Like it was a dream and he a phantom.

I'll wait for him to come to me again and then maybe I can find out if he had been here with me last night. Surely I couldn't have dreamed all of it. Surely.

But I know that he loves you too, as do I,

Your loving mother,

ML

# Chapter Thirteen

*"I am a feather for each wind that blows."*
*-William Shakespeare*

March 12, 1982

Dearest Perdita,

𝓘 used to have dreams for my life. And they began to come true. I was climbing that ladder and, although it's hard to believe now, I was something big once. People loved me. I was a "new talented voice" that rang out from radios all over the world. I was on T.V.

I was especially big in Europe. I traveled through Europe opening for the band Starkiss.

I'm long forgotten now. I had sent my agent away. I heard the band has a new lead singer now. You see, when someone disappears, everyone forgets. I was dispensable. I guess that's just how this music world works. You can't stay on top for long and there's always someone there, waiting for their chance to step onto your stage.

When I look in the mirror now, the face I see contains nothing of those former days. My voice is cracked and unused, so different from the notes that used to peal out. I wish I could touch my guitar and strum it, feel strings beneath my fingertips. I long to play music, but not nearly the way I ache for you.

I used to imagine us singing together, me on the guitar and you nearby, our voices melding together. We'd sing the songs you'd learn at preschool like "wheels on the bus" or "eensy weensy spider." I can imagine your small fingers twisting around each other and working their way up the spout, until your arms reached over your head. On top of the world.

I hoped for so much, but now I'm wasting away in this room. This morning, I asked the hands with my breakfast tray for my guitar. Said she'd look into it. It's almost lunchtime. Maybe she'll bring it along with the salad and the pills. It's not much to hope for, but it's all I have. If only I could feel the weight of my guitar against me and pluck out that melody that once brought me success, brought happiness into the world. My hands would be busy, moving, strumming, not idle as they are now, hovering and waiting.

Maybe someone would hear my song through a crack in the window and remember. Remember that I once was more than this washed-out nobody without enough hope, or strength, to even climb out of bed. Peeling paint on a forgotten door.

Maybe someday the sun will come out. I wish your father would be the one to dig out my old guitar and bring it to me. Maybe he'd ask me to sing for him. He'd asked for that song that drew him to me at first. Maybe he'd remember how much promise I once had and remember our love that created you, and I'd once again be the woman I was meant to be:

Talented,
Beautiful,
Unforgettable,
MonaLee

## Chapter Fourteen

*"Like a bank, for love to lie and play on;*
*Not like a corse; or if, not to be buried,*
*But quick, and in mine arms. Come, take your flowers:*
*Methinks I play as I have seen them do*
*In Whitsun pastorals: sure this robe of mine*
*Does change my disposition."*
*-William Shakespeare*

"Can I use your laptop?" Phil asked, looking up from the letters. "I have an idea."

Piper slid the unused laptop across the table to him.

She ignored the tap, tap, tapping of his fingers as he typed and didn't look up again until music played from the computer. It was an older song that sounded familiar, but Piper didn't really know how she knew the song. She must have heard it on the radio from time to time.

"It's 'Let's Play in Love,'" Phil said. "MonaLee's song."

"The MonaLee? The mother?"

"This is like the real deal, Piper," Phil said. "I'm not sure how you got these letters, but MonaLee really was a famous musician. She was some sort of one-hit wonder."

"Maybe the media's done a 'where are they now' segment on her, like that show they have on VH-1?"

"Let me see," Phil said and started typing again.

Piper couldn't just sit there reading about accounting when MonaLee's life was materializing on her laptop screen. She wouldn't have thought she could use her computer to find stuff like this. I guess it made sense. She used it for researching papers and such. Of course, there would be information on MonaLee if she really had been a famous musician. Piper slid her chair over to Phil's so that she could watch the screen.

Phil clicked on a photo with the words, "Where is MonaLee now?"

Piper read aloud the sentences that stood out. "Famous pop star of the early eighties, most famous for her song 'Let's Play in Love,' has been battling drug addiction for years. After marrying up-and-coming, politician Leo Stately, politics running heavily through his veins from the time of his great, great grandfather, MonaLee was expecting her first child at age twenty-three. When that child died soon after birth, MonaLee spiraled down, using drugs to deal with grief and depression. Her mental health has never recovered and her husband Leo cares for her in their Concord home. She never wrote another song."

"Because they won't even let her have her guitar," Phil said. "Sounds like she would have been better off in a mental institution."

It was true. MonaLee was suffering from drug addiction, which Piper knew from the letters. Only it wasn't the type of addiction everyone thought. And the poor, loving husband was her jailor.

Piper reached over to see the photo of MonaLee more clearly. She was a young, pretty, dark-haired girl with bright, blue eyes and an "on top of the world" smile. She looked exhilarated with life. She was holding her guitar in her arms as if it were a baby. The song was playing from the computer. Her voice, mingling with the guitar, rang out like a musical thread of silk.

Piper wasn't sure what it was she felt in her apartment as she listened, something like home but more tingly like excitement. She knew something the rest of the world didn't. About MonaLee. *What was she supposed to do with this information? And how, oh how, did these letters come to be in her possession? What would this old pop rock star have to do with a viola?*

The music was strangely haunting and familiar. When the song finally ended, Piper felt a possessive pride for her. Embarrassed, she wiped tears from her eyes.

"She really was amazing," Phil said.

Piper nodded her head and felt guilty. Here she was, hiding and refusing to play music while MonaLee would have done anything to play that song again, any song. Piper had the freedom to walk out her door and play for the world, yet she was hiding. With more than a little fear, Piper stood and went to the corner, lifted her viola case.

"Let's do this."

\*\*\*

They plowed through the snow and ice blanketing the sidewalk, under the lamp posts and Christmas lights. They found a corner near a popular deli that served imported coffees and cocoas. People were dining inside, talking and laughing and sipping from their mugs and espressos. Outside, more were clustered, wrapped in their coats and scarves, waiting for lights to change and hanging around just a bit longer. It filled her with a nervousness she hadn't felt since the last time she played for a group of people—since the audition—and her heartbeat quickened as she opened the case and pulled out her bow.

Her hands shook as she rosined her bow, but the shaking was for so much more than the cold she felt.

"For MonaLee?" Phil asked.

"For MonaLee."

Phil handed her the viola, then set the opened case before her, a vessel for spare change. She smiled hesitantly and put the instrument up to her chin, the bow to the strings. She had planned to play one of the pieces she had prepared for the college audition but her fingers had a mind of their own as they began to play her song, the melody from her dreams. She played and the notes filled the street.

She forgot herself and where she was; she forgot about being afraid, and she played notes laced with love. With unrealized hopes still lurking amongst phrases. She thought of MonaLee begging for her guitar and tried to pour forth a melody to calm her fragile soul, wherever she was. Piper closed her eyes, and the music took over.

When she reopened her eyes, a small group of people had gathered around. Crumpled dollar bills and a puddle of change lay in her outstretched case, the silver reflecting the lamplight. More people were looking out the deli window with interest. She took the viola from position, then bowed her head shyly and smiled. The small group clapped a steady wave of admiration.

"Will you play something more?" an older woman asked. She had a beanie pulled well over her head and held a Styrofoam cup in her gloved hands.

"Anything you want me to play?" Piper asked. It had been so long since she'd performed, but from the time she was a child, she had been able to play any melody she wished.

"Jingle Bells?" the woman asked.

Piper nodded, put the viola to her chin, and played a version of Jingle Bells, filled with broken harmonizing chords and set in a minor key. She played it slow and melancholy, as her mind drifted to a distressed MonaLee alone on Christmas Eve. With no one to love and no baby in her arms. She was nearly overcome with the sadness that rang like lonesome bells from her bow against strings. She felt MonaLee within her. It wasn't like Piper to become emotional when she played, but she felt sadness weighing her down. When Piper looked to the woman who'd requested the song, she was wiping a tear from her face.

The woman stepped toward Piper and put a hand on her shoulder, "You have a gift, my dear." The woman stooped to drop a ten dollar bill into the case, smiled again at Piper, grabbed the hand of a man she was with and crossed the street. Things had settled back down in the deli and most of the crowd had ambled on.

Piper looked to Phil where he sat on a bench beside the viola case and said, "Did we get enough for some firewood?"

"Do you really need to ask?"

Piper gently set the viola into its case and pulled out the change and bills. Amongst the jumbled offerings lay a folded sheet of paper.

"I wonder what this is," Piper said, holding the paper up to Phil.

"Maybe some practical advice." Phil shrugged. "Don't eat yellow snow?"

Piper shook her head and laughed. "Very funny," she said, and unfolded the lined page. Words were scribbled haphazardly, not within the tidy narrow lines, but diagonally and messy.

Piper read aloud to Phil.

*"I remember you. You auditioned at the university last spring. You have a great gift—I saw it then and it's still with you. I want to explain that it would be a lot of work, some technique and form would need to be reversed and fixed. You might have to start back at the beginning and it wouldn't be easy, but you have the music in you. It's not something I see every day or in every musician. Sometimes it's easy to miss it when we're so stuck on bow grips and form. But it's important to fix these things so that you will be taken seriously as a musician. You could be brilliant. I have a full roster this year, but will fit you in if you decide you'd like to give it a try. Erica Jaschine, Professor of Viola Studies, 555-8461."*

Piper looked up. "It was the woman from the audition. Did you see anyone writing?"

Phil shook his head.

Piper folded the paper back into its creases and slid it in her coat pocket along with the cash. She held on to its bulky hope as she walked home, arm in arm with Phil, stopping at the corner store for firewood.

The fire cracked and glowed in the hearth as Piper lay in Phil's arms, both outstretched on the sofa. She felt as if she'd overcome some kind of personal roadblock tonight and wondered if maybe, just maybe, it wasn't all over for her after all. *Could she still make something of herself with music?* But every time she let her mind wander down the long, echoing halls of the music building at the U, she shook the idea from her head. Then she thought of the way the people had looked at her tonight, as if she were special and the way Phil saw her, and everything seemed okay. Maybe she could go back, maybe she could call this Erica woman and give it a try. Piper leaned into Phil's chest and watched the flames and felt a moment of absolute perfection. She rolled over and faced Phil. From his eyes, she wondered if he could feel the same.

She put her hand to the side of his cheek and smiled at him. "Thank you," she said, in a whisper. "For making me do something that makes me happy. And for making *me* happy."

She leaned into him and began to kiss him. It was so warm in his embrace near the fireplace and as they kissed, things were getting even hotter. Piper wasn't experienced—not at all—but maybe this was the moment and maybe Phil was the one. She pressed her body up against him and felt as though she was ready to give everything to him. *But how would she compare to someone like Summer who knew exactly what she was doing?* The thought of Summer made Piper feel much less bold. It was just at that same moment that Phil pulled away.

"Piper," he said, shaking his head. "I want to do this right. Let's not rush."

Piper closed her eyes, nodded her head in the niche of his neck, and agreed. She hid her flushed cheeks beside him and was relieved. Piper was glad he'd been the one to slow things down, because she wasn't sure she'd have been able to.

***

*A*s Piper slept in Phil's arms that night, she drifted into another dream. She sat at a wooden table in an unfamiliar, formal dining room with tall windows and extravagant draperies. A large fire burned in the fireplace. Piper was bent over a pad of paper, doing accounting problems. That's when she heard the crying—the heaving familiar sobs. Piper stood up and followed the sound. As if in a trance.

The room led into another room, what looked like a parlor, with expensive furniture and tables. The house was a huge labyrinth, room after room, with the sound of sobbing still far off. She followed the sound down a long corridor lined with portrait paintings, like something out of old British estate houses. She looked to the portraits and saw the tear-smeared eyes of the same woman in each. The paintings were impressionistic and blurry. The sobs turned into the music, the quivering sounds from the recurring song in Piper's dreams. When she was sure she found the door, she pressed her ear to the wooden frame and listened. Yes, this was it. She twisted the knob and pushed the creaky door open.

In the middle of an elaborately detailed, Persian rug lay a puddle of a woman, head down and crying, her dark hair swimming in a pool of blood that had soaked the rug.

Piper rushed to her, "What's wrong? What can I do?"

The sobbing ceased. The woman slowly looked up, pushing her hair, dripping scarlet blood, from her face, the tear-stained face of Mona Lee.

***

*O*ver breakfast the next morning, Piper told Phil about the disturbing dream she'd had, about the blood and the face she now recognized after all those years of having this woman visit her dreams. Phil was eating a bowl of breakfast flakes at the table.

"I just feel like I need to do something," Piper said, between bites of oatmeal from a mug.

"You do know she has no idea who you are," Phil said.

Piper nodded. "It's crazy, isn't it? Maybe I could tip someone off—the police? Or even a woman's group?"

Phil shook his head. "I think the police would blow you off. It's like calling the police and saying you have inside information on the life of the president. They'd probably chalk you up as crazy."

"I know," Piper said. "Maybe I just need to know if MonaLee's still in trouble. Maybe she's not. Maybe there's no reason to worry."

"You could try to contact her," Phil said, after refilling his bowl with cereal and adding more milk.

*Could she? Would she be able to reach some Senator and his washed-up singer wife?*

"I know I had no business even reading the letters, but they fell into my hands and, yeah, maybe I will. I think I have to try to reach her."

Phil said, "Although, you might not be able to reach her if she's held captive, but with a famous politician like her husband? You should be able to reach him somehow. You could do another computer search."

Piper nodded and lifted the lid of her laptop, which was sitting beside her on the table. She set down her oatmeal and typed *Leo Stately* into the search engine.

"Okay," she said. "He's the U.S. Senator of New Hampshire. There's some sort of page here where you can 'Contact your Senator'."

"There you go," Phil said, adding another spoonful of cereal into his mouth.

"What would I even say? Hi. You don't know me, and neither does your wife, but she needs my help? By the way, stop drugging her—and she'd really like her guitar."

Piper shook her head, laughing, while she pulled up the contact information. Despite how ridiculous this seemed, it was something she needed to do. It seemed awkward and hopeless and strange. *Piper had enough sense to realize MonaLee's face in her dream wasn't really a warning? Was it?* Nothing felt sure anymore. Still, it bothered her so much that she felt she had a duty to try and help her. What Piper couldn't wrap her head around was the blood. *Why had MonaLee been wallowing in blood? Was her husband going to hurt her? Had he already?*

Piper read through a couple more pages with Leo Stately's name attached to them. She perused a couple political columns insinuating that he would he would be America's answer to problems if he would run for president.

"President? Of the United States? Really?" Piper mumbled her thoughts aloud. "I guess it doesn't take much anymore."

"Our Leo Stately?"

"Well, he's not running or anything, but these people seem to think he should. I'd hate to see his dirty laundry aired out to the public." Piper said, "That would be ugly."

Piper went back to the *Contact your Senator* button and pressed it.

"Okay, here goes nothing," Piper said, to Mopsa who was wound up into a furry ball on her lap. "I should send something, right?"

"It can't hurt," he said. "What's the worst that could happen? He doesn't respond."

She typed out a quick message. Piper was sure it would enter into a virtual slush pile that some intern would pick through amongst letters from other concerned citizens about new laws and state budget issues.

"What would I even say?" Piper asked Phil, as he was rinsing his bowl in the sink. "I can't tell him the truth. And I don't want to alert him that I know something I shouldn't. That could put MonaLee in even more danger than she's already in."

Piper shrugged. "Maybe I could say I'm a cousin of MonaLee's and I need to talk to her about some private, family business. A death, perhaps?"

"A will with her name in it? Money might intrigue a senator to respond," Phil added.

"Not a bad idea," Piper said, as she began composing a letter:

*Dear Senator Stately,*
*I'm not just any ordinary citizen, but I hope you can help me. I am the cousin of MonaLee, your wife—*

"What's MonaLee's last name?" Piper asked Phil as he pulled his chair next to Piper's so he could look at the screen. "Wait, what if MonaLee isn't her given name?"

"Like Madonna," Phil said. "Is Madonna's name really Madonna or is that a name she chose herself for her image?"

Piper looked at him and cocked her head. "I think Madonna is her given name. If I really were MonaLee's cousin, I would know. But you know, MonaLee *did* sign her name to the letters some of the time."

"You could just use Stately as her last name," Phil suggested.

Piper nodded and continued typing.

*—Stately. My cousin and I lost touch quite some time ago, but I need to contact her and am not able to do so. My family does not have any current contact information. We have lost our dear Uncle from a stroke—*

"Stroke," Phil said. "Nice touch."

"Is that vague enough?"

"It's good. And instead of money, maybe you could make that more of a mystery too."

"Like a family heirloom?"

"Sure."

*—and it appears MonaLee's name is on the will. He has left her a valuable, family heirloom that we in the family would like to see make it safely into her hands. Please contact me immediately to let me know how I may be able to do so. You may call me at—*

"Do I leave my phone number and address? And how am I to sign this letter?"

"Just get the letter out there," Phil said. "If she doesn't recognize the name, she might not care. Maybe it will be a way for her to contact the outside world, and that will be enough."

"Either way, it's worth a shot, right?"

"Right."

*—529-555-7809. Time is of the essence. Thank you for your help, Carol*

Piper looked to Phil, who nodded, and then Piper hit send.

"Now we'd better get going."

As Piper climbed into Phil's SUV, she thought back on the letter she had just sent out into this invisible, cyber world. It made her nervous, and she felt strange knowing that she could maybe help. She thought back on the letter and realized that she had inadvertently infused the letter with some of the formality of MonaLee's letters to embrace that almost mature tone she'd become accustomed to. Piper wished that MonaLee would have mentioned a cousin but in thinking back on the many letters she read, any mention of people in her life was vague and never specific or by name. Piper knew it was a long shot. But it was exciting to have Phil on her side with this. Like they were a team.

## Chapter Fifteen

*"I am bound to you:*
*There is some sap in this."*
*-William Shakespeare*

𝓟hil gripped the steering wheel with Piper at his elbow as he drove the icy overpass into the mountains where he was to drop Piper off at her car. He was tired from very little sleep the night before. He and Piper had talked the night away, sharing whispered words, until they had silently nodded off. It had been perfect, the kind of night when you bare your soul to the one person in the world who gets you. She was soaking him in and the more she did, the more she seemed to melt down too. He'd never had anything like this with a girl before, when he'd rather learn what was going on in her head than how he was making her body feel. A tiny feeling had popped into his heart as he listened to her talking—about *what* he couldn't even remember—that maybe this is what love was. The kind of love at the end of girly sappy movies where the guy's darting in and out of traffic, rushing to get to the one person who makes him whole. It was ridiculous, really. He scorned these cliché romantic movies where the guy needed to get a grip on it, man. And that's what Phil was telling himself: Just get a grip on it, man.

But there was something stirring inside of Phil that made him antsy and excited at the same time. He could hardly breathe. His knuckles were white as he gripped the steering wheel.

"Are you okay, Phil?" Piper asked, from the passenger's seat where she had looked up from studying. It seemed like she always had a book in her lap or hand anymore. Phil knew that Piper was stressed about end-of-term. She cared a whole lot more about school than Phil had when he was there. She placed her hand on his arm, as delicate as a butterfly landing. *Okay, dude*, Phil told himself silently, *get a grip.* He squeezed tighter on the steering wheel until his shoulders began to ache from tension.

"I'm good," Phil said, looking back to the street before him.

"Do you want to know something weird?" she asked.

He nodded.

"Last night, you know, when we were talking. I felt I'd known you forever. When I talk to you, it feels therapeutic and safe. Like I'm writing myself down into a locked diary. I know that sounds so dumb. I should really just stop talking—"

"No, don't—" Phil said, "—stop talking. I do know what you mean. It doesn't matter what I say; you will accept me. Like, my whole life, I was getting ready to meet you."

"You feel it too," she said and smiled, her blue eyes warm. Her hand was still resting on the back on his arm.

Phil now knew he wasn't making this up. Maybe he shouldn't squelch the idea that this is what love felt like, so different from his experiences with girls up until then. Where they were waking up together but didn't know what was happening inside their heads. And really, he hadn't wanted to know before. Still, Phil couldn't help but feel sappy and unmanly. *Was love supposed to feel like an opening of souls and pouring from one to the other?*

He had spent two nights with her and hadn't slept with her. It didn't seem rational. Not that he didn't want to sleep with her, he just didn't want to screw things up by doing something she would regret. And he'd never had to do much before—as soon as the bedroom door shut, whatever girl he was with was pulling off his clothes and hers. Summer had been like that. It had been so easy with her. It's not that she wasn't nice. She was, and he'd liked her as much as the next girl. Really more, she was cool and could ride a snowboard like no girl he ever met before. Plus, she was hot.

Piper didn't have that same quality, the type of hot that all his friends could see. But that was good. He didn't want anyone else to find the treasure she had hidden beneath that pom-pom hat of hers. As they pulled onto the ski resort exit, Phil abandoned all hope of regaining his composure. He felt like he would burst if he didn't say what he felt. It was all pent up and, with each passing second, building momentum. Hopefully, he would feel relief when he finally released his thoughts. Especially when she would tell him too that she felt the same way. Like a coming together of hearts.

"Piper," he began. "Before I drop you off, I have to tell you something." He paused and took a deep breath. He'd been told by girls that they loved him and he'd only responded with a casual "Yeah, me too." But he'd never said the three words to them or instigated all this love stuff. He said it so he wouldn't lose the high of it all.

"Yes?" she asked.

They were stopped at a red light, so he looked over to her. "I've never met anyone like you." Okay, now it was coming out like some sort of sappy, marriage proposal. Redirect, Phil told himself.

"What I'm trying to say is that," Phil took a drink from a bottle of water. "I think I love you."

Phil looked at her. Her eyes were round with what looked like surprise.

The silence felt so heavy, and his heart was beating so hard in his chest it felt like it was banging to get out. He was worried she might hear it and know he'd never done this kind of thing before. It's like his heart was beating the sound of pounding feet, running through traffic and rushing to catch her just in time before she stepped on that plane to Paris or New York or wherever those girls in the chic flicks are heading. The light turned green, and he stepped on the gas.

When she didn't respond, he looked over to her. Her mouth was open, like she was not sure what should come out. "Thank you."

His heart nearly stopped. He had told her he loved her. She was the first girl in his life that he'd said those three words to, and she said "thank you." Wow. That was anti-climactic. It wasn't the type of response the guys in the chic flicks ever got. No, they always flung their arms around their guy, and there were tears and happiness and long, deep kisses. Music swelling.

In her defense, he was driving and there would be no long kiss here. Still, he felt shaken and rejected and ultimately unloved.

She tried to say more. "Phil, I think you're great. I just—"

"Please, don't," he said. He didn't want to know what she was going to say—I just don't love you yet. I just don't think you're *that* great. I just don't love you at all. Phil didn't want to know.

They sat the rest of the drive in silence. When they reached the parking lot, the tow truck was already there pulling Piper's car from where it had been stuck the last two days. Piper thanked him in a shaky voice, kissed him quickly on the lips, and then scrambled out of the Pathfinder. He was relieved she was gone.

***

*A*s Phil turned the car around in the snowy lot, he curved a little too fast—so glad to be done with the gone-all-wrong moment—and found his wheels spinning on the snow-packed ground, his tires squealing like releasing the pressure of the last five minutes. He fishtailed and then righted his steering wheel and sped off.

When he opened the door to his apartment, Tommy and Zane were ready to head out for work, coats on. Summer was eating a bowl of cereal at the table, which struck Phil as a little odd, but he didn't ask. He just nodded to her. He figured out pretty quickly who Summer was there with though, as Heath said he'd be riding to work with Summer. Heath could have her. Although it did seem to be an extra jab on what was now turning into a pretty crappy morning.

It was slow on the mountain that day. He spent the morning up in the Eagle Lookout lift shack and did a lot of shoveling the ramp. He needed to exert his frustration somewhere, so why not take it out on the snow? In midmorning, when the phone rang in the shack and Tommy called up to tell him the boss said they could take the rest of the day off and go riding, Phil didn't hesitate. He would snowboard his day away and forget Piper. He didn't want to sit around all day and overanalyze why she'd said what she said and wonder if she truly didn't feel what he'd been feeling. He felt like an idiot. *Why had he told her he loved her after like, two days of being together?*

That night, Phil's friends were having some people over and it turned into some full-fledged party. Phil had been to parties with these people before and knew what it would be—a lot of drinking and maybe some weed. Phil didn't get into the heavier stuff that he knew was there too. That wasn't his thing.

He sat around a table in the kitchen, playing poker. He needed the distraction. The music was loud, the cigar smoke was heavy and hazy, and he won himself a hundred twenty-five bucks.

Sure, there were girls around—of course Summer and her friends, some other girls who worked in the restaurants and other parts of the resort, even some local girls from Park City. None really tempted him. In fact, in light of what had happened that morning, Phil was glad the smoke was so thick he didn't really have to look at any of them. One of the girls from Park City, some young red-haired girl who looked like she was still in high school, had come over to him, all flirty-like buzzing around him, but he just shooed her away. Summer was a little more difficult to get rid of. *If she was supposed to be with Heath now, why did she keep making her way over to him?* He'd had her, done that already. Still, as the night grew on and the beer soaked into his brain, he thought about how nice it was to have someone to go home with and not have to play any of these head games.

At one moment, Heath was sitting next to Phil and as if she was trying to be closer to Heath, Summer squeezed herself onto his seat, whispering and laughing with the guys. A little irritated and relieved, Phil shifted over, making more space for her so that she wasn't sitting in his lap as she'd nearly been. Finally, after his final game of cards, with the winnings in his pocket, Phil got up and wandered through the crowded house. He ended up on the sofa, watching TV through the haze, until he fell asleep. He awoke a little while later, not really sure how long he'd been out on the couch, and the room was almost empty. He stumbled through the house to his bed.

***

The next morning in the lifty lodge, Phil was assigned to Hellacious, the top-most lift at the resort. Pretty fitting lift name considering the way he felt after last night. It was quiet up there as the only runs down were black-diamond to "you better have life insurance because chances are you'll biff so hard you'll die" runs. As Phil turned to pack away his stuff in the locker, Heath asked, "Dude, will you switch lifts with me?"

He shrugged. "Which lift?"

"Frozen Tempest," Heath said. "Dude, look, Summer's got the morning off and I want to work somewhere more—secluded. She's gonna come *visit*. Plus, it's windy. There's a good chance they'll shut it down this morning. Please, just for the morning."

"It's all yours," Phil said. Phil wasn't sure why this bugged him, but whatever. Good for Heath. *Why would he care?* Still some part of him felt like he'd lost all of his options. Phil grabbed his snowboard, his only constant lately, and began to walk off.

"I didn't bring my long board today, and the pow is crazy up there after the dump last night," Heath yelled over. "Can we switch?"

"Dude? Anything else you need? My kidney? The shirt off my back?"

"Chill," Heath said, catching up to him. "It's just for the morning."

"If you so much as put a scratch on it—"

"I won't. I probably won't even leave the shack this morning. I need it just in case. You can come up and get it after lunch."

Phil petted the ocean waves printed on the front of his board as if it were a live thing and handed it to Heath, carefully. He clutched Heath's board, the yellow and black Skate Banana, under his arm as he walked away. This worked out anyway. Phil didn't mind using the Banana in the half-pipe at Frozen Tempest.

## Chapter Sixteen

*"I cannot speak
So well, nothing so well; no, nor mean better:
By the pattern of mine own thoughts I cut out
The purity of this."*
-William Shakespeare

That morning, after Phil sped off, Piper drove home and inwardly cringed at how she'd handled Phil after his declaration of love.

She'd been feeling it too, something amazing that was playing between them, and yet she couldn't reciprocate. *Why couldn't she have just said it too?* Three words. "I love you." She sensed it too. She'd even thought about those three words—I love you—before he'd said them to her. *So, what was the matter with her?* She just didn't have a whole lot of experience with this kind of thing, and it just felt strange. To just come out with it and admit it. She still wasn't sure why her heart was thinking, "Yes, I love you too," while her mouth could not say the words to him. *And, now, what was he thinking?* It was too painful to think about. She would have to think about something else.

School.

Piper had been putting it off for far too long. After all, it was crunch time. Studying would be a nice distraction, as long as she could keep her thoughts on accounting.

As soon as Piper drove into the valley, she would head to class and then spend the evening cocooned in her apartment studying and finishing her term papers. And, if she focused on her schoolwork, maybe she could erase those ridiculous words—"thank you," really?—she'd said at least momentarily and feel less like a fool.

Later that evening, after a day full of reviews and study sessions in the university library, Piper sludged her way through the snowy parking lot back to her apartment, cold wet snow seeping through her jeans into her socks. As she entered her apartment, Mopsa and Dorcas were, as usual, mewing as though they hadn't eaten in a week.

"Okay, okay," she said, as she shut the door behind her on the frosty night air. "I'll get you dinner." She kicked off her shoes by the back door and entered the kitchen.

As Piper filled the cat bowls, she noticed the blinking light of her answering machine. Maybe Phil misses me already, she thought, hoping he'd left her a message so they could work it all out. Maybe he'll even come down again tonight. She hoped that she hadn't turned him away after this morning. But as much as she wanted him to spend another evening with her, Piper knew she needed to focus on her finals.

Unfortunately, it wasn't Phil. She pressed the button to hear an unfamiliar, very professional man's voice on the machine. She forgot to breathe and felt jittery all over as she heard the deep voice say, "Carol. My name is Leo Stately. I received your email and would like to speak with you. Please call me directly at 495-555-6290."

Piper took a deep breath, picked up her phone, and began dialing. *And what was she planning to say?* I mean, there wasn't an actual family heirloom and she wasn't really MonaLee's cousin. She hung up before the phone began to ring. Okay, let's recap here. I am a cousin of MonaLee's who's lost track of her. My name is Carol. From the letters, it appears that MonaLee hasn't had visitors from anyone at all so it shouldn't be odd to have lost track. Her uncle has died recently and left her a family heirloom. I need to get it to her. That's all. *Wait, where do I live?* It can't be close to them. I'll say I live here so that

I'm far enough away that I'm safe and can't stop by this afternoon. *How would her husband know where the relatives of the family have moved since they were married, right?*

She picked up the phone again, dialed, and waited with a shaky hand holding the phone, while it rang once, twice. "Leo Stately speaking."

"Uh hello, Senator Stately. My name is Carol. I am a cousin of your wife's." She tried to make her voice sound as old and mature as possible, when she heard her young feeble voice entering the phone. *She felt silly. This whole idea seemed ludicrous as she was now speaking to an actual Senator on what can only be his private line and what could she possibly accomplish with this? How could she have taken it this far?*

"Carol," he said.

It startled Piper that his cold, professional voice turned warm when he said her name. As if he knew which cousin Piper was pretending to be, maybe he thought he'd chatted with this cousin Carol at his wedding or at a family gathering in the past. Or maybe it was his "everyone's important" political voice. Either way, Piper would play along.

"I was hoping to speak to MonaLee," Piper continued, not really sure how to respond to his apparent change in demeanor.

"She's... unavailable. Do you know that MonaLee's been very ill for many years?"

"I've heard that, yes," Piper said, trying to sound informed.

"And I'm afraid she's gone."

"Gone?" Piper asked, her heart seeming to stop. *Could she have died? Was it too late?*

"She's left," he said. "I don't know where she's gone. I was hoping maybe back to family?"

"I... We haven't heard from her." Piper said, still playing the part.

"If you do, I hope you'll let me know. I'm worried sick about where she could be. She needs the best medical treatment in her condition, and I'm worried what might happen to her if she doesn't take her medicine."

He sounded phony to her. *And why was he acting so warm and loving? How could he possibly know Carol?* She didn't exist. Plus, Leo himself was what had caused MonaLee to stay so sick. Medicine, right. She knew what was in those pills. She wanted to call him out on this but couldn't.

"Of course."

"I mean that. Please, if you know where she is, please contact me."

There was something about the tone in his voice in his last plea that sounded desperate. Maybe he was sincere. Maybe MonaLee had escaped. And perhaps she had even found breadcrumbs that led her to her daughter, Perdita.

As Piper got off the phone with Leo Stately, she promised to keep his number and call if she found out MonaLee's whereabouts. She wanted to tell Phil—her partner in all of this—what she learned.

She picked up the phone again, still warm, and began dialing Phil's number. It went straight to a voice message. It was just as well. She really needed to study for her final exams. Only two "study" days left, a weekend, and then finals week would be in full swing.

Try as she might, with all those books and notes and papers spread out before her, her mind kept drifting back to the phone call with the Senator and how she needed to tell Phil what she'd learned. He wouldn't believe this tasty bit of information she had. Piper checked the clock. It was nearly ten-thirty now, several hours later than the last time she tried to call.

Piper closed the cover of her textbook and decided there was no way she could study anymore. Not tonight. Not with this information. She picked up the phone and dialed Phil. Two rings, then Piper stood up, frozen as she heard loud music thumping in the background and a girl answered in a sing-song voice.

"Hello. What can I do you for?"

Piper was too startled to speak at first.

"C-can I talk to Phil?" she stuttered.

The girl cackled. "Ewww. I don't think so. Hey Heath, you haven't seen Phil. In the bedroom? With who? Really? Yeah, he can't come to the phone right now. He's *busy,* if-you-know-whatta-mean."

Piper hung up. She couldn't stand to listen to her any longer. She felt hollow and sickened.

In her panicky state, she jumped up from the couch and began putting things in order—straightening up in the kitchen where she'd left hurriedly that morning, put her boots away, swept the stray pieces of cat food back into the bowl. Her hands needed to be busy to calm her. She used to find solace in her music. Maybe she would try that to relax her. Oh, but it was after quiet hours. Sometimes Piper hated having all those restrictions on her.

Still, she opened her case and stared down at the sleeping instrument, thinking about the last time she had played, outside in the frosty night air, and remembered Phil and MonaLee. Piper settled into bed and thought of the way she felt that night, how she felt her music could reach the world. It had reached Phil. She wished she could call out to him tonight. She wished he would call her. She turned onto her side and stared at the silent phone sitting on the bedside table. Still and calm, as she wished her heart could be, but it seemed to be beating so laboriously and hard it just might leap from her chest. Oh sleep, please come, she whispered into the darkness.

***

𝒯he next morning when Piper walked into the lifty lodge fifteen minutes late, it was nearly empty. She checked the chart, Snow Hare as usual for her. She also made a mental note that Phil was assigned to Hellacious. Piper wouldn't be able to find Phil right away, but maybe she could use a break in her morning to go see him and tell him what she'd found out about MonaLee. He needed to know this. She also wanted to tell Phil that she was sorry about yesterday, that she needed him. Now more than ever. And that she did love him.

Around ten-thirty, she explained that she needed to take an early lunch break and her "relief" came—a girl named Daisy—to staff the shack while she was gone. It wasn't easy to get to Hellacious. She would have to take several different lifts to get up there. Piper was second-guessing herself for never learning to ski or snowboard. At least lifties were allowed to ride the lift back down. She trudged through the snow to Frozen Tempest where Zane was checking lift tickets and manning the loading dock.

Piper considered asking him about Phil, but decided against it. *Zane seemed nice enough, but what was there to say?* Plus, he was doing the job two people would normally be doing and probably didn't have time for chit-chat. She smiled at him and hopped on the lift, pulling her signature hat down over her ears to stay warm against the cold wind. At the top of the lift, Piper looked into the lift shack and recognized Tommy. She lifted her glove in a slight wave and he slowed the lift so she could hop off without skis or a board.

She had a short walk over to load the lift at Hellacious. The packed snow helped with the long hike to the next lift. Phil wasn't working the bottom of Hellacious so she assumed he was in the shack up top. She said a friendly, "Good morning" to Gayle, a skier who had two long braids dangling from the sides of her beanie. Piper spoke briefly with her from time to time. Gayle was cool, down to earth.

"You headin' up?" Gayle asked.

"Yeah, I need to talk to him," Piper said, and gestured to the top. She sat as the lift seat scooped her up.

"He's a popular guy today," she said, then waved. Piper wondered what Gayle meant. She would have asked, but she was already headed up the lift with Gayle still down below.

Although it didn't take long for Piper to realize what Gayle meant. For as Piper had reached the top of the lift, there was no one there to slow it down for her. Leaned up against the shack were two snowboards, Phil's blue ocean waves, next to a pink smaller board. Piper strained to see inside the window of the lift shack, searching for Phil, but became startled when she witnessed what could only be Summer's long, blond hair cascading over Phil's shoulders. Piper stared open-mouthed at the scene of Phil making out with Summer right there in the shack for Piper and anyone else riding up the lift to see. Piper bumped her head against the inner pole, dislodging her pom-pom hat. She grasped for it with her shaky, useless gloved hands as it landed with a soft thud onto the ramp. At least she was able to hold on to the lift pole as the chair jerked around the turn, headed back down the lift.

She looked in the shack again—how could she not?—and Summer looked up at her, seeming as startled as she was. Piper turned away, but not before locking eyes with her.

As Piper rode back down the lift, she pressed her head into her gloved hands and cupped her warm breath around her frozen *face. How could he? How could Phil be with Summer? After everything that they'd had together, after what he'd said to Piper only yesterday?*

Piper headed straight to the lifty lodge and talked with Neil about taking the rest of the day off. She told him she was sick. And sick she was—her startling realization affecting her physically in a way she didn't realize it could. Her body was shaking and felt warm, almost as if her body temperature had skyrocketed despite how cold it was today.

Now it was all fitting together. It especially made sense of the girl answering the phone last night. He had been with Summer last night too. She had turned him away, not reciprocating his confession of love, and now he'd turned back to Summer. Maybe he'd never stopped with Summer. Maybe Piper had been some sort of game to him all along.

Piper drove home. She would study all afternoon. When she entered her apartment around noon, the answering machine light was blinking. It had to be Phil, but she couldn't talk to him now. And she didn't want to listen to any excuses that would break her heart. Summer had probably told him that she had seen them.

She kicked off her boots and jacket. She opened the refrigerator, not because she was hungry but because she didn't want to look at that blinking light. Her stomach was still upset; there was no way she could eat right now. She filled up a glass of water, drank it and sat down, her stomach queasy. She stared at the blinking light and walked zombie-like over to it, pressed the button. Her finger had a will of its own.

But it wasn't Phil. The message contained her mother's voice, frantic and scared, calling from Minnesota.

"Piper? Oh Piper, you're not home. I need you. I have something to tell you. You must call me right away. It's about your father. I'm waiting."

As soon as she heard her mother's anxious voice on the message, the pit of her stomach grew—the kind of pain that means your life is changing and can't ever go back.

She took a deep breath and dialed her mother.

"Hello?" her mother's voice came through the line after the first ring.

"Mom, what is it?"

"Oh Piper. I should have told you before. I was waiting until you came home for Christmas, but I don't think there's time. Your father's been diagnosed with cancer."

"No," Piper said, collapsing into the cushions of the couch.

"It's renal cell cancer. The doctor told us at the end of August. He said your Dad had only six months to live. I knew it couldn't be true. I thought for sure that he could pull through, that if I prayed hard enough God would give me a miracle and let him stay. But he's gotten worse, so much worse."

"Mom, you should have told me," Piper asked, slumping over. *The end of August?* Piper wanted to scream, cry at her mother for leaving her in the dark like this. But she couldn't lash out at her mother as much as she wanted to. She could hear the pain in her mother's voice. She knew her mother had carried the pain for Piper so that she could continue being a kid and a student. "I could have come home and helped. What kind of treatment has he had?"

"He's been doing chemotherapy, but it's made him so sick. He's not eating. He's been asking for you. Especially on the days when he feels more lucid. I've been putting him off. I told him you'd be home soon. Couldn't he wait just another couple of weeks?"

"Mom, I need to see him."

"I know, honey. I hate to pull you away from your first semester. I want to make sure your plane ticket home is as soon as you can possibly leave after your semester ends. That's why I'm calling. I need to change your ticket right away."

"My finals are next week," Piper said. "Thursday morning is my last test. Can you get the ticket for Thursday afternoon?"

"Yes, of course."

"Can I talk to Dad?"

"I'm afraid he's sleeping. He hasn't been well these last few days. His lucid moments are becoming fewer and fewer."

"How's Clint doing with all of this?"

"He's having a hard time. He helps me move Dad around the house. He's been home a lot. I don't know what I would have done without him."

"I'm surprised Clint didn't tell me," Piper said softly, to herself really. She trusted Clint and they talked all the time. He was the one person she could count on to make her feel at home without the pressure of doing everything just right.

"I asked him not to. I really felt that your father's health would turn around, and he would begin to heal."

"No, I can't wait. I need to be with Dad. Can you get my flight today?"

"But all your work would be wasted. A whole semester of work, not to mention the tuition, all for nothing. You don't want to start off with a semester of incompletes, do you? He'll be okay until you return, I know he will, but he needs your prayers."

"Of course, mom. I still wish you had told me before."

"I'm sorry, Piper. I was trying to help."

"I should have been told."

"You're right. He's *your* father. Listen, I need to go and change your flight. Plan on Thursday. I love you, Piper. So does your father."

"I love you too, Mom. And will you please have Dad call me the next time he's awake? I need to make sure he knows how much I love him."

"Yes. I promise. Goodbye."

"Goodbye, Mom."

Piper placed the phone back and sat still, staring ahead at the blank white wall, immoveable. Piper felt heavy, as though a house of bricks weighed down on her. *Why hadn't her mother told her right away?* Piper tried to imagine him. She conjured his face. He was always there for her, for her brother and mother, always putting them first—before work, before anything else. She was his *star*, he used to tell her.

Piper flipped through old memories of her father, reaching as deep into her childhood as she could. She was walking down Main Street with her father, hand in hand, wearing a little blue dress, the one with the rhinestone belt, and lacy socks. Her mother had made the dress. Daddy marched her to the store, his eyes sparkling like the rhinestones. Piper's mother told the story a handful of times, always saying, "He was so proud of his little girl with the dark curls and bright blue eyes."

And then there was the day he had brought her the viola, the very first one in the beat up case. The way he hid it behind his back and then offered it to her, smiling a little sadly.

"I wish it were exactly what you wanted. I hope a viola is okay," he had said to her. Piper remembered squeezing between him and the old case.

"Oh Daddy, of course. You've made me the happiest girl in the world."

The day she left for college, he wouldn't let her go.

"Dad, it's time. I have a long drive ahead," she kept telling him.

"Just one more hug." And it would start all over again. And she'd feel safe all over again in her father's arms, before she had to make her own way in the big world she thought she knew but would soon realize she didn't. And that it was lonely being so far away from her family, the only people in the world she could count on to be on her side.

When she arrived at college, she felt alone, just another person going from class to class, from school to work and back again, not making much of a difference to anyone.

Until Phil came along. He seemed to care more about her than the rest of the world. But he hadn't really. She knew that now. No one here cared about her. Piper needed someone to hold her, someone to listen while she spoke about her dad and death and this ugly world she didn't understand. *So why did she wish for Phil now? Even after his betrayal?*

Piper looked to the stack of books mounted on her kitchen table, with papers and notes scattered. And all she could think about was her father. Her dying father. No, he couldn't die! Piper couldn't imagine him sick. He'd always been healthy, always doing something, fixing something around the house or working out in the yard, getting up early to jog several miles before work, but then taking a short "rest" on the couch before going in to the office. Although he had a soft spot for sweets. Piper knew, as a child, she could always convince her father to get her some ice cream after dinner or get him to open a bag of chips in the afternoon. She smiled, knowing she could always count on him that way too.

She smiled just at the thought of it, then her smile grew heavy with the realization of what her mother had said, that he wouldn't eat anymore. This wasn't her father. *How could this have happened to him? Why her family?* The one thing in her life that was constant.

Piper couldn't wait. She didn't care about school or finals or Phil when the one person she needed to see was miles and miles away and every ticking minute was another minute away from her father. She didn't try to talk herself out of it. She packed up a bag. Tucked the note she kept by her bed into the folder of her viola case. And reluctantly, her cats. Stuffed them all in her car. She didn't care about her job or her finals. She was going home. Tonight. She needed to be with her father. Nothing else mattered anymore.

## Chapter Seventeen

*"She prizes not such trifles as these are:*
*The gifts she looks from me are pack'd and lock'd*
*Up in my heart; which I have given already,*
*But not deliver'd. O, hear me breathe my life..."*
*-William Shakespeare*

*O*n slow days like these, the guys tried to get in as many runs as they could. Phil rode up the lift pretending he was letting the guy working the upper lift take a break for bathroom or coffee or whatnot. That's what he'd tell the boss, if asked, anyway. He, Zane, and Tommy had been playing at this relay game all morning, taking turns, riding their snowboards back down through the half-pipe, handing off the metaphorical baton to the next guy. It sure made the workday a lot more bearable.

At lunch break, after a quick bowl of soup at the cafeteria, Phil trekked over to Snow Hare, hoping to get a glimpse of Piper. He wasn't feeling quite as raw as when he'd last seen her—it's amazing what a little time, a couple drinks, and some snowboarding will do for perspective. When he couldn't find her, Phil shrugged it off, wondering if she had been assigned to a different lift or maybe she was at lunch although he hadn't seen her in the cafeteria where she usually ate. *Could she have taken a day off?*

After eating lunch, he called Piper's apartment but got her recorded voice. Phil hung up, choosing not to leave a message. With everything kind of weird as it was, he wanted to talk to her for real to feel things out. He had been putting off returning the calls she'd left for him over the last day and a half, since she thanked him for saying 'I love you.' But he'd shaken off the hurt and now he was ready. He decided he'd call her later and didn't think much more about it.

Phil went up the Hellacious lift to relieve Heath for his lunch break when he noticed Piper's hat, the unmistakable green and blue pom-pom hat that Piper always wore, lying at the edge of the ramp, pushed out of the way, a little trampled and half buried in snow. Phil took off Heath's snowboard he'd ridden all morning, left it against the shack, and went to pick up the hat.

"Was Piper here this morning?" Phil asked, as Heath came out of the lift shack.

Heath looked at the hat and shrugged. "I didn't see her."

Phil wiped the snow from the hat protectively. "Hmm... okay," he said. "See you after lunch. Tear it up." Heath binded into his own snowboard and cruised down the mountain.

Phil carried the hat into the lift shack. It didn't make sense. *Piper didn't ski or ride, so why would she have been up here?* Unless she lost her hat and someone else was wearing it. He placed it onto the counter and resolved to return it later that day if he saw her. Or he'd drive it to her tonight.

Phil turned on the CD player in the shack, randomly playing songs from Bob Marley's Greatest Hits. The CD had always been there. He wasn't sure who it belonged to, but he tapped his fingers along with the beat and sang along a little. "Don't worry about a thing." He placed Piper's hat on the counter. "Cause every little thing's gonna be all right." He kept singing, trying to keep away the jittery thoughts from not knowing where Piper was. Despite the upbeat Reggae music filling up the shack, he still felt sick to his stomach.

"No Woman, No Cry," came on next. Phil stared out the window watching empty ski lifts pass by one after another.

He stood. The poem! The verse he'd added to, scratching in a line of his feelings, cementing how he'd felt about Piper before his feelings avalanched him. Phil turned around, aching to get another fix of Piper. There it was, his heart scratched onto the wall of the Hellacious lift shack:

*Love is a secret, snowflakes falling in the dark.*
*At light, I realize it's covered me.*
*Swallowed me.*
*Am I still there when the storm's passed,*
*after the thaw?*
*Or am I a deadened remnant of something that never was?*

The last line was new—and followed the bit Phil had written a while back. He sat there, looking at the script, the handwriting that appeared to match the first line he'd originally discovered on the wall. It seemed curvier, definitely a girl's handwriting.

*Who would have done that?* Summer? Surely not Piper. Had she added that line in light of *recent developments* and then forgotten her hat? Phil didn't understand poetry really. It was vague and carried feelings with words he didn't fully understand. Words that flowed on the edge of what was in his head and his heart. Still, he couldn't help but feel that last line was a dig on him. *Was someone saying that this new thing Phil felt wasn't really him?*

Phil turned around, looking out to the snowy, white expanse seemingly deserted now and his fingers itched. He thought of the way he'd told her he loved her. He had meant it. But the look in her eyes—skittish like a bird that could spread out her wings and fly off at any moment—made him wonder if she didn't believe him. As if it was something he had said many times before, but he hadn't. It had been the first time he had felt love for anyone spilling out of him through his words. His heart started beating again so heavily he had to pick up the pencil that was pinned to the clipboard. He turned around and kneeled, adding more:

*Foreign and new,*
*re-shaped with you inside me,*
*frozen in my heart.*

His heart had changed since meeting Piper, after she tracked her prints all over his heart, trampled all over who he'd been. But it was okay. He was a better person.

Phil rode his snowboard down the mountain, fast and a little out of control, with Piper's hat stuffed into his pocket. The huge pom-pom dangled outside, not willing to be contained inside the zipper. As he rode past the rental building, Summer was locking up. She turned around as Phil's momentum slowed. He stooped to unbind his foot from the board and Summer was walking toward him.

She gestured toward the bright blue-and-green pom-pom.

"Hey, sorry about that," she said.

"What?"

"I'm not sure why she looked like that," Summer shrugged, acting all nonchalant and shit. "Like she saw a ghost or something."

"What are you talking about?" Phil asked.

"I'm not sure *why* she was riding up the lift to Hellacious this morning. No one usually comes up Hellacious on the really heavy powder days since so many people have gotten stuck up there. I swear we hadn't seen more than five people all morning. If we had known we'd have a visitor, we would have been more discreet."

"We?" Phil asked. He stopped walking and was digging the edge of his snowboard into the snow. "You mean Heath and you?"

"Let's just say she came up at a really inopportune moment—well, not for me, but for her," Summer said, smiling smugly that made Phil want to punch something.

Piper thought *he* was with Summer. "No, no, no. Heath had my snowboard," Phil said, turning away.

"Listen," Summer said, clutching onto his arm. "I know what she thought. I tried to find her, to tell her it wasn't you but she had already gone. Neil said she went home sick."

"No wonder," Phil said, shaking his head instead of finishing his sentence. He had to get a hold of her. He had to explain.

"Look, there's something else," Summer said, her eyes downcast. "I'm sorry about all of this. Last night, at the party, when she called. I didn't know where you were but she may have gotten the wrong idea. It was supposed to be funny, but I can see now how maybe it wasn't. I really am sorry."

"I've got to go," Phil said, and took off for the lodge.

"Sorry," she yelled after him.

When he got home, Phil called Piper's number over and over and over. Just getting her recording. Of course she wouldn't pick up her phone. She probably never wanted to see him again.

After he change clothes, he drove the thirty minutes to her apartment, but she wasn't there and neither was her car. He sat on her back step. He even pressed his ear up against the door trying to glean the sound of the cats inside meowing or padding through the apartment. The windowsill where one or both the cats usually sat was empty. Not one light was on, not even her small Christmas tree she usually kept lit from the window. It didn't make sense. Still, he would wait for her. And he would explain it all. It was dark and cold outside. Phil sat hunched over, trying to keep in any warmth he had remaining, and watched the headlights of cars passing. He stared across the old, chain-link fence over to the park on the right. The lamp posts reflected light and the snow made the night seem a little less like night. A full moon hung overhead, like the globe pendant light hanging in his room back home. The park was nearly deserted but for the occasional dog or two doing his business. The park benches were piled high with snow. After nearly an hour, as Phil was considering getting into his car and heading back home, a small white truck pulled into the lot. Not Piper. An older man with a handlebar mustache climbed out. He was walking across the parking lot when he saw Phil.

"Can I help you with something?" he asked.

"No, well, maybe," Phil said, so unsure about his words or anything anymore. "I'm waiting for Piper. She lives in this apartment." Phil gestured to the door behind him.

"You're going to be waiting a long time, my friend," the man said. "She left today. I don't know when she'll be back, but it ain't gonna be anytime soon."

"Left? Where did she go?"

"Home." The man was just a foot away. "I wouldn't normally know this kinda stuff. Piper keeps to herself mostly. She called me this afternoon and told me she was leaving for a while. Going home."

"Home—like as in Minnesota?"

The man nodded.

"Do you know how I can reach her?"

"Look here. She's my niece sorta, and you seem nice and all, but how do I know she wants you to know where she is? Huh? If she wanted you to know, she'd have told you."

Phil shook his head. "Please, sir," Phil said, hoping to throw in some formality to show he was a decent, respectable guy and not some crazy stalker or punk who would do Piper any harm. "She's angry with me. She left so suddenly that I didn't have time to straighten things out." Phil shook his head, more slowly and sad now, to himself. "I can't believe she left because of me."

"What's your name?" the man asked.

"Phil."

"Well, Phil," he said, placing his hand on Phil's shoulder in a paternal sort of way. "Don't be so hard on yourself or *full of yourself*. It wasn't you. Her father's sick. He's my cousin, you know. She went home to be with him. Your *little misunderstanding* may have been fodder, but she went home to be with her family."

"Maybe you could just give me her number in Minnesota?"

"Sorry, kid." And with that, the man went to an outdoor shed wedged between the fence and Piper's back door and pulled out a snow shovel.

Phil wasn't about to give in this easily. Here was someone who knew where Piper was. Phil followed him and said, "Need a hand?" If there was one thing Phil felt was his territory, it was snow shoveling.

The man looked back at him, shrugged, and handed him the shovel, then went back for another for himself. "You can leave me your number, if you want, and I'll get it to her."

"She won't call me back," Phil said. "We had a sort of misunderstanding." The man didn't respond so Phil began shoveling. There was something comforting about the order of pushing unwanted snow away. He had gotten used to molding and organizing the matter of snow, and it seemed to clear his head.

Some of the guys at the resort even began sculpting animals out of the mounds of extra snow they shoveled out of the way. The tourists began taking their pictures with the snow-sphinx that had been Phil's brainchild. It was quite good, Phil couldn't help but admit.

Phil decided he'd rather be slaving away shoveling with Piper's second cousin or third or great uncle—he wasn't sure how all this worked. It was better than being stuck in his apartment thinking of Piper and not knowing how to get to her. *What other option did he have?*

Amidst the sound of shovel scraping against ice and the concrete below, they talked.

"Are you originally from here, uh—" Phil asked.

"Blaine's my name. I'm not from here, though my wife is," he said. "Not sure how they do it, but they're always luring you back to where they come from. You from these parts?"

"California," Phil said. "My buddies and I came here for the mountains."

"You're in the right place. The skiing is like no other. And the snow—well, there's a lot of it," Blaine said, as he continued plowing through with his shovel.

"Shouldn't you have one of those snow blower things?" Phil asked.

"It's in the shop, so I figured I'd have to come here and do it the old-fashioned way. It's nice to have some help."

"I do this kind of thing all day long at the resort in Park City," Phil said. "That's how I know Piper. We work together."

He stopped shoveling and shook his head. "It's tough, what's happening in Piper's family," Blaine said. He dug his shovel into the ground and leaned on it. "Robert's a good guy. I hate to see him going through this."

"I'm surprised Piper never mentioned it," Phil said, and stopped shoveling as well.

"I don't think she knew, to tell you the truth. The rest of the family's known for quite some time. They were trying to protect her."

"How bad is it?" Phil asked.

"I don't think he has long."

Phil stared at his feet. "Piper," he whispered and then looked back up to Blaine. "This is going to destroy her."

"He doted on her," Blaine said, and he began shoveling again. Absentmindedly, he said, "They were so alike you'd never realize she was adopted."

Phil had picked up his own shovel and was about to dig in again, when he stopped.

"What's that?"

"Oh, well, uh," Blaine stuttered. He looked baffled and wasn't sure how to proceed. "I, uh, was just saying how much he loved Piper."

"And that she wasn't—his biological daughter?"

Blaine continued digging, determined, as if he could shovel his last words away.

"Was Piper adopted?" he asked.

"I guess I probably shouldn't have mentioned that little tidbit."

"*She* never mentioned it."

"*She* doesn't know," Blaine said. "It was so long ago. I nearly forgot it was supposed to be some sort of secret. I trust you won't say anything about this. An old man like me lets things slip now and then."

"I didn't think people did that anymore, not tell their kids when they're adopted," Phil said, thinking aloud more than actually talking to the old man. He looked over toward the park and noticed a solitary person sitting on the bench closest to the chain-link fence. It was odd considering how much snow there was, and the form was alone, not with a dog or anything. *Why would anyone be at the park on a snowy and cold winter night?* He turned back to Blaine.

"Okay, look here, I'll give you the address and phone number if you'll give me your word you won't mention that little detail."

Phil was torn. While he felt he had to be loyal to Piper, he just had to get to her soon, so that he'd have a reason to be loyal to her. He had to get that address.

"Sure. You have my word."

Blaine held out his hand in an old-school show of agreement and Phil shook it, cementing his end of the bargain.

After they finished shoveling the lot and the sidewalk, Blaine scribbled Piper's address and phone number on a slip of paper. While Phil was pulling his Pathfinder out of the parking lot, he noticed the woman still sitting stock still, a statue, with the moon's light reflecting off the snow like a spotlight aimed right on her.

***

After Phil returned to his apartment and hastily packed a bag, he dialed the Minnesota phone number Blaine had given him. The phone rang three times before a guy's voice answered.

"Hello?"

"Hi, um," Phil stuttered, not sure how to put this. "I'm a friend of Piper's. Is she there?"

"Nah man," the voice said. It was a young voice. Definitely not Piper's father, maybe her brother's? "She's away at college."

"No, I know that," Phil said, and shook his head at how difficult it was to spit out the words he needed to say. "I am a friend of Piper's from college, but I hoped she might be there."

"No, not yet. She'll be coming home next week for Christmas break."

"I thought she might have come home early."

"Nah, sorry."

Phil realized that, of course, she wouldn't be there yet. *How long does it take someone to drive to Minnesota from here?* Many hours. He had no idea but obviously her family didn't know Piper was on her way home.

Phil knew what he had to do. He felt unstoppable and like a man on a mission. He had to go to her, all the way to her.

Phil explained to his slightly disgruntled roommates that he'd be gone for a couple days, grabbed his bag of clothes and stuff, and walked out the door.

He climbed into the driver's seat and gripped at the cold steering wheel. He took a deep breath, readying himself for a long journey at the end of which—Phil hoped—he would deliver himself to her, to show that she was worth the journey to him.

## Chapter Eighteen

*"Your sorrow was too sore laid on,*
*Which sixteen winters cannot blow away."*
*-William Shakespeare*

𝒫iper pulled off at an exit to fill up the gas tank. As she waited at the pump, she put her hand onto the hood of her car to encourage her old, but reliable, car to keep going. It was going to be a long night and by her calculations, she wouldn't arrive until right before sunrise. Hopefully she wouldn't startle anyone when she opened the back door (surely the key would be where it's always been under the rock). She envisioned her parents waking up to find her on the couch in the morning.

She hadn't called home ahead of time. She didn't want her mother to try to talk her out of returning. *What were tests anyway when your father was dying? What did accounting and British Lit matter in the huge landscape of life when it might be irretrievably altered?*

Piper fluffed up a couple blankets in the back seat for Dorcas and Mopsa to rest comfortably. Piper listened to radio stations when she could get them, always seeking out a classical station that would soothe her heart. Or calm Dorcas who was meowing in a low anxious timber she'd never heard before. The viola rode next to her in the front seat, and as she listened to static shifting between radio airwaves, her fingers ached to the touch strings. She reached out and rested her hand on the leather case. A relief swept over her just knowing the viola lay inside, as well as the offering of a future in music. After a while, Dorcas climbed over the console and nudged her head under

Piper's hand. The cat settled down into Piper's lap as she scratched under her chin.

She drove for hours and hours, two headlights pointing toward home, toward comfort and indisputable love.

At one in the morning, her car found the driveway with her old, basketball hoop. The house was dark, compared with the Christmas lights outlining most of the neighbor's houses up and down the street. Her house looked so forlorn.

Piper struggled carrying the cats and walked around to the back of the house. No lights were on in the small shed that housed Mom's sewing studio either. Piper found the spare key safe and sound as she expected. Once safely entrapped in the backyard fence, Dorcas sped off into some bushes. Mopsa seemed frightened and pressed her head into Piper's armpit. Dorcas would have to be okay inside the fence. She was the wild cat who had always tried to escape. She'd be fine.

"It's okay, Mopsa," Piper said. "We're home now." She fumbled with the lock until it clicked, and she stepped gently inside and closed the door. The cat jumped down.

The medicinal smells Piper encountered upon entering didn't match up with her memory of home-cooked meals and her mother's scented candles. Piper found a steel, metal bed in the center of the living room where the round coffee table once stood. She could hear her father's labored breathing. On the couch, nearby, her mother was clutching her bed pillow in her arms as she slept.

Piper tiptoed to her father. The man who was stretched on the bed was a much older, thinner version of the father she had left behind just four months before. His nose seemed bigger and his skin stretched like wax over his forehead and jutting cheekbones. Her fingers traveled over the white sheets to where his bony hands rested. If it weren't for his slight chest movement, she would think he couldn't possibly be alive. *How could this be her father? How could this broken body hold all the love he had shown year after year?*

Piper pulled her hand back. As quietly as she could, she went to Clint's bedroom, where he lay asleep on his bed.

"I'm home," she whispered, and then tiptoed to her bedroom and collapsed onto her childhood bed, weeping. She needed to get this out now so that she could be composed and put together later today when he was awake, when it would actually matter.

Piper wasn't sure when her sobs turned into sleep, but they did and she found herself in the early morning light with Mopsa's warmth curled beside her. Her mother was brushing Piper's hair from her face, where it had stuck against her cheek.

As Piper's eyes adjusted to the morning, she smiled.

"You came," she said.

Piper sat up and wrapped her arms around her mother's neck.

"Is he awake?" Piper asked.

"Not yet," her mother answered, sweeping Piper's hair behind her ear as she had done when Piper was small. "Soon."

Piper's mother led her into the kitchen and began pulling out several cereal boxes from the pantry. As she set the boxes on the table, she looked Piper up and down, shook her head.

"You must be starved. You're so thin."

"No, mom. I can't eat now. How am I supposed to eat?"

Her mother set a bowl and milk on the table and she said, "Piper, I'm already fighting your father about food. Don't make me fight you, too. Now, what kind of cereal do you want?"

Piper obediently sat down and shook Cheerios into the flowered ceramic bowl with the chip. It amazed Piper how much fondness she could have for a bowl. Her mother followed up with the milk jug. There was something soothing about being back at this table, being taken care of. She jumped up when she heard the sound of quick steps coming downstairs.

"Clint!" she said, in an excited whisper, standing.

Clint hugged Piper, nice and long. Piper was shocked by how much her arms had to stretch to get to his shoulders. He had grown so tall and broad in the last several months. Clint's shaggy brown hair hung in his eyes and Piper reached up.

"Are you under there?" she asked.

He jerked his head to the side with a practiced movement, which pulled the hair from his eyes. She could see big brown eyes. He was the same, old Clint. Her kid brother she was so happy to see. She hugged him again.

"When did you get here?"

"Late last night," Piper said, as she sat back down to eat her cereal. "I drove straight through."

Clint joined her at the table. "I'm so glad you're here. We need you." He began pouring his own bowl of cereal. He turned to look at his mother who was holding out the milk jug. "Is Dad up yet? I can help him to the bathroom before I leave for school."

Mom handed him the milk and peered around the corner to the living room. "He's not up yet, dear. But you go. Piper can help me today."

Clint nodded. He finished eating in what seemed like record time, interrupted with short bouts of bantering and current happenings in his high school world, and made for the back door with his backpack slung over one shoulder.

"We get a cat?" Clint asked, as he opened the back door, where Dorcas was waiting. Mopsa darted outside as Dorcas came in. "Two?"

"I brought them," Piper said, leaning down and plucking a very cold Dorcas from the ground. "I couldn't just leave them in my apartment. I'll see you after school."

Piper went to take Clint's bowl to the sink. It still had a thin layer of milk at the bottom so she set it onto the floor for Dorcas. The cat lapped while Piper went quietly into the living room. She would sit near her father until he woke. One of the kitchen chairs was set up nearby, and Piper pulled it close to the bed. She watched him for a while and when she felt her eyes starting to fill, she laid her head on the bed near his arm, trying to feel his warmth. After several minutes, Piper felt the sheets rustle. She lifted her head and was looking into the eyes of her father. He didn't smile—it was almost as if it would take too much energy to do so—but his eyes shone in a way that Piper knew meant he recognized she was there and was glad of it.

Piper held back an impulse to fling her arms around him. He seemed so fragile.

He took a deep breath. "Piper. My beautiful daughter." He had to pause between each word, but it was so good to hear his voice. He was still there underneath everything she didn't recognize.

She smiled and gently pressed his hand. "What can I do for you? Do you need something to eat? Or another blanket? Do you need to get up for anything?"

His eyes shone. "No."

Piper's mother came around the corner with a cup and spoon. "Time for breakfast," she said, in a cheerful voice. Piper wondered if her mom talked to her dad this way all the time, as if she hadn't noticed his body's deterioration. She probably thought that if he didn't realize he was dying, then he wouldn't.

"I have something you can do to help. You can help Dad with his breakfast smoothie."

"Of course," Piper said, taking the cup before her mother disappeared back into the kitchen.

Piper dug a spoonful of the smoothie and slowly brought it toward her father's lips. He didn't open his mouth. She waited a minute, and he slowly shook his head.

"I can't," he said, his voice breaking.

"You don't want to eat?"

"No."

Piper lowered the spoon back to the cup and stirred it around a little. "What kind of smoothie is this?"

"A bad one," her father said and broke into a weak smile. He was still funny.

Piper took another spoonful and brought it to her nose. It had a strawberry-like smell but was also earthy and metallic.

"Oh Mom," Piper called to the kitchen. "What are you feeding Dad?"

"It's just a strawberry-banana smoothie," she said, looking around the corner. "He likes them."

"This is just strawberries and bananas?" She held up the cup.

"I may have added some extra nutrients to give Dad a little protein. You can't even taste it."

"Mom, I can *smell* it."

"I only added a little."

"Okay," Piper said. She placed the smoothie cup down on a side table.

"Do you really not want any?" she whispered to her Dad.

"It makes me sick," he said. His voice was lowered as if he didn't want Piper's mom to hear him.

"You've been eating for her, even though you don't want to?"

His eyes were intense. Piper could tell from those eyes that he knew he was dying. He knew his body was rejecting the food because it had no use for it.

"I won't make you eat if you don't want to."

"Thanks," he said, and patted her arm with his frail, bony fingers.

"Could you handle some ice chips?" Piper asked.

He nodded.

"I'll be right back," Piper said, and squeezed back his hand gently. She padded into the kitchen and filled a cup with crushed ice from the refrigerator door.

Her mother was standing at the sink, her hands immersed in bubbly water, but stone-still, looking out the window.

"He needs to eat," her mother said softly, defeated. She didn't turn around when she said it.

Piper set the cup down and wrapped her arms around her mother's shoulders from behind.

Her mother rested her cheek on Piper's arm and they stayed there like that, a statue of embrace, for quite some time. It wasn't just her father who needed her right then. *Why hadn't her mother called Piper sooner? How could she have done this all alone?*

Piper spent the morning at her father's side, spooning ice chips into his mouth, napping when her father napped, speaking in hushed voices with her mother about her father's hospice appointment, and food. It felt strange to be this still, when the last several months of her life had been a whirlwind of work and classes and Phil.

Phil seemed like a distant memory within these familiar paisley walls, among people she loved more than anything. She wanted to forget about Phil. She imagined him off with Summer now; she couldn't quite get over the hurt she felt when she thought of him. She had let him in— into her apartment, her life, her heart. It was like her life had expanded to let him in and now that he was gone, the hollow spot ached for him.

Piper looked up as her father awoke from his nap. She could hear her mother bustling about in the laundry room. Her father's eyes were serious. She could tell he was trying to speak. Piper held his hand to encourage him.

His words, when they came, were slow.

"I waited." He breathed several strained breaths and continued. "For you."

Piper's eyes stung with the onset of tears. "I came as soon as I could."

"You should know," he stopped and swallowed. Piper scooped some of the watered-down ice into the spoon and offered it to him, but he shook his head. "I never regretted. The deal. We made."

She offered him another spoonful of ice and he took it.

"You are. The best. Daughter."

"Oh Dad," Piper said, tilting her head toward him aching to hug him. *What in the world was he even saying? What deal? With God?* Her mother had told her earlier in the kitchen that sometimes he talked nonsense, especially lately. That he had some lucid moments, but mostly he didn't seem to know where he was or who he was. He'd even spoken to non-existent people he thought were standing beside his bed—an old, army buddy who had died beside him in Vietnam, his own dead father, some childhood friends. But, still, it felt like what he was trying to say was important. Maybe she would ask her mother about it later.

After a while, he spoke again. "I wanted. You. To know. The gifts. Weren't. From us."

Piper shook her head, confused. She'd just continue to show she loved him and nod her head as though she understood these perplexing words. She gently stroked his age-spotted, wrinkly hand. A hand that should have belonged to a ninety year old, not her father who was only sixty.

"Dad, I love you."

"They called. You. *Perdita*."

"What did you say?" It couldn't be. How odd to hear that strange name from her father's chapped lips. Piper's head started to spin and she tried to be patient while he labored on. *Someone called her Perdita? Who?*

"We called. You Piper."

"Yes," Piper said. Maybe her ears were playing tricks on her. Surely he couldn't have meant to say Perdita. *But why Perdita? And how could he have known?*

"I can go now," he said, and closed his eyes.

The well in her eyes began to overflow. "Please don't, Dad. I'm not ready to lose you."

He rested his head back against the pillow and closed his eyes. He sighed from what seemed to be exhaustion. Piper pressed her wet face into the blanket beside him.

She closed her eyes and wondered what it could all mean. *Did he know something about MonaLee and her daughter Perdita? Or was this just a coincidence? Could he have been saying that she was Perdita, the stolen baby from the letters?* But that was impossible. Her life hadn't been the life of a child stolen from her mother. That simply wasn't the life she lived. Piper tried to draw from memory the years of MonaLee's letters. Her parents weren't capable of such an act. They were kind and normal. Normal parents don't steal babies. Piper tried to think through this logically. Maybe it was all just a coincidence. The name. There had to be other people with that name in the world. In her fuzzy consciousness, Piper tried to block the whole crazy idea from her brain.

Piper felt pressure on the back of her head. She had drifted off again, so sleep deprived from last night's long drive. It was her mother. A nurse, frumpy wearing blue scrubs and holding a bag of equipment, stood behind her.

"Darling," Mom said. "Hospice is here."

Piper released his hand. But it seemed different. Piper stood and knew right away, as the nurse searched for the heartbeat that there wasn't one.

The nurse lowered her stethoscope and said, "I'm sorry. He's gone."

\*\*\*

𝒫iper sat on the porch swing, zombie-like, pushing back and forth with her foot on the ground. She felt chilled from the frozen wood of the swing through her sweatpants. She watched the puff of her breath as she released it, focusing on the back and forth of the swing, and the in and out of her breath.

It was all too soon. *Why did he have to go so soon?* She had just gotten there. And his puzzling parting words seemed to have meaning. Piper tried to remember every detail of the conversation. His last words had indeed been that he was ready to go. Now *that* she knew. But she wanted everything clarified, and the person who could do it was no longer there. His words were so strange. "The gifts weren't from us." *What could that have meant? What gifts?* They called you Perdita. There were too many coincidences. Piper wanted to know what it meant. Maybe her mother knew.

After a while, the front door opened and closed. Her mother waited until the swing hit its peak and she sat down beside her. Piper wanted to ask her mother about the last words, but she didn't want to worry Mom. Maybe it would all make more sense if she just talked to her now. But somehow it didn't feel appropriate.

As she was debating how to broach the subject, her mother spoke.

"You haven't eaten," she said. "Do you want me to fix you something?"

"I'm not hungry, Mom, please just sit with me for a while." Piper placed her hand over her mother's. The swing creaked its rhythmic pattern.

They swung, staring out and listening to the swing creak *back and forth, back and forth*. After some time, the sound of tires on gravel mixed with their creaking swing and her mother looked off toward the driveway.

Piper and her mother continued their trance-like swinging. Piper knew people were coming to take her father's body away. She refused to look over. She didn't want to see strangers carrying him out of her life forever. It had to happen, but she didn't want to see it. Just keep swinging, she thought.

The door burst open and Clint appeared. His hair was covering his eyes, and tears coursing down his cheeks. Piper and her mother both moved from the swing and met Clint, the three of them with arms intertwining, and heads tucked into necks, a convoluted embrace. Clint's rawness gave way to Piper's and her mothers. They openly wept.

After the heaving hushed, the three settled back on the swing.

"How did he go?" Clint asked.

"It was peaceful," Piper said. "In his sleep."

He nodded, seeming relieved. "Did you know?"

Piper shook her head.

"He was waiting for you, Piper," her mom said. "He was holding on until he saw you one last time."

"He missed you so much," Clint said, and hiccupped another sob away.

Piper put her arm around Clint. He was cold, like she was, but she pressed her side to him for warmth as well as comfort.

"I missed him. I missed all of you." Piper pulled both Clint and her mother in for another hug. "I just wish I could have had a little longer with him, but I'm so glad he waited for me."

When the front door swung open, they watched silently as Piper's father's body was carried out on a stretcher with a thin blanket outlining the contours of his thin frame.

\*\*\*

*A*fter hospice packed up the hospital bed from the living room, the three of them spent a quiet afternoon holed in the house, reminiscing and laughing and crying. Piper and Clint played Scrabble in front of the hearth, just like old times, while their mother phoned relatives and visited with neighbors and friends who had heard the news and showed up on the front door stoop with food and flowers. Being home felt right, as if Dad were smiling down on them. After a while, Piper settled onto a corner of the couch, curled herself up with a blanket, and took a nap.

\*\*\*

*P*iper walked along a busy, downtown street with so many strangers pushing and rushing ahead. She didn't know where she was going, but she seemed to be in a hurry to get there. A dark-haired woman ahead of her moved with *click-clacking* heels and had a green, leather purse flung over her shoulder, which seemed to push her off-center, as she struggled to keep moving forward. Piper recognized the face of the crying woman from her recurring dreams as she passed her by. She tried to say hello to her but the woman looked confused as she did, as if they didn't speak the same language, or maybe it was just a vacancy in her eyes.

Piper kept walking, still intent to get where she was going. She heard a scream peal from the woman, that familiar cry, and turned back. The woman was struggling with a man for her purse. The man was yanking on the strap while the woman clung to it. Piper tried to weave through the sheep to turn back and help the woman. Piper tried to scream to the thief to leave, but her voice was empty and her words lost. As she reached them still scuffling over the purse, Piper yanked onto his arm and he finally let go. The purse fell to the sidewalk along with the woman. The woman wrapped her arms around it as though it were a living thing and rocked it in her arms to soothe it. The man didn't run off. She was looking into the face of her father.

Piper began to ask why, but he smiled at her and opened his arms to hug her. She looked to the woman who had stood, wrapped her arms around the purse as if it were a baby, and began to *click-clack* off. *Click-clack-click-clack.*

It took Piper a moment to realize where she was in the darkness of the room. *Click-clack.* It was a knocking on the front door. *How long had she slept?* Piper pushed Dorcas from her lap to answer the door.

When she saw Phil framed inside the front door, she opened her mouth to speak but found nothing would come out, a continuation from the dream. *How could Phil be here?* His eyes were sad, mirroring her own. Here he was, this boy she never wanted to see again but also be with every minute of her life.

Piper stood in confusion. The idea of her Phil, from so far away, standing here on the porch of her childhood home in Minnesota seemed impossible. *And how could he have known she needed him so much at this very moment?*

Her heart took over her head as she rushed to him and put her arms around his neck, tears welling her eyes.

"Why are you here?" Piper asked, relieved to have mastered the art of speech again.

"I had to see you."

Piper's mom looked around the corner from the kitchen.

"Piper?"

"Mom, Phil is a friend of mine."

They pulled away from each other.

"I'm Piper's mother. Please invite him in, Piper," she said, disappearing back around the corner. Piper stepped back to let him inside and shut the door.

"I'm sorry, Piper. I'm so sorry. About everything."

Then the realization of why Piper had felt so betrayed came rushing back, and Piper fought between her head and heart and shook her head.

"Aren't you with Summer now?"

"What you saw, it wasn't me. I tried to call you, but it was too late. You were gone." Phil reached his hand out to her, but she pushed him away.

"No, I saw you. I saw your snowboard. I saw what you were doing."

"You didn't see *me* with Summer," Phil said, his voice low. "It was Heath. He was using my board. He needed a powder board. That's all." Phil held out her hat that he still had tucked into the pocket of his coat. "I found this and knew what you must have thought. *Heath* is with Summer. Not me."

"But the phone call—"

"Summer was playing a stupid game. I could never be with her. You've got to know that. Not now that I have you—or I did."

Piper shook her head. "No," she said, so softly he leaned in closer to hear her. "The way it made me feel—like I was some sort of beggar, waiting for more. I won't let you make me feel that way again. I trusted you."

"Piper," Phil said, putting his cold hands to her face, but then he pulled them away when she shivered. "You *can* trust me. I won't let you down again."

Another question was on Piper's lips, but the sound of a glass shattering in the kitchen silenced her.

"Mom, are you all right?"

She left him framed in the doorway and ran to the kitchen where her mother was already cowered on the floor, sobbing over broken pieces of glass.

"Mom," Piper said and tried to pick her up. "Your finger. It's bleeding." She led her to the sink, and turned on the tap to run warm water for her mother. As the water streamed over her hand, the blood trailed down the drain.

"I'm sorry," she said. "I'm so clumsy."

"You've been through so much," Piper said, and pulled a clean dishtowel from the drawer, wrapping it around her mother's hand.

Piper led her to a chair at the kitchen table to sit. "I'll come back and clean it up."

When Piper turned the corner, she said, "I can't do this. Not right now. My dad just died, and I can't deal with this too. You need to go."

"Please, don't send me away," Phil said. "I came so far."

"You shouldn't have. I can't just forget how you hurt me," Piper said, and stepped past him to open the front door. A gush of cold air rushed in. She wished she could just forget. *She wanted to have him there and not to have to do this alone, but how could she ever trust him?* He didn't leave.

"I've got to go," she said, and turned. "Shut the door on your way out."

It wasn't until she began sweeping the shards of glass into a pile that she felt the front door snap shut.

## Chapter Nineteen

*"What you do*
*Still betters what is done. When you speak, sweet*
*I'ld have you do it ever: when you sing,*
*I'ld have you buy and sell so; so give alms,*
*Pray so; and, for the ordering your affairs,*
*To sing them too: when you do dance, I wish you*
*A wave o' the sea, that you might ever do*
*Nothing but that; move still, still so,*
*And own no other function: each your doing,*
*(So singular, in each particular)*
*Crowns what you are doing in the present deeds,*
*That all your acts are queens."*
-William Shakespeare

𝓟hil hadn't considered being turned away. He hadn't thought, during the whole nineteen hour drive, that his going there wouldn't be enough to show how much he was into Piper. In his head, he stepped out of his car and that was that. He was forgiven.

*Now where the hell was he to go?* He was in a state where he didn't know a single person except one, and she didn't want him there.

Phil tried to swallow the lump in his throat. He walked away from her door, climbed into his car, started up the engine and put his hands in front of the still-warm, heating vent. He needed sleep. He'd go somewhere to sleep and think things through with a fresh mind. He backtracked through the street that had brought him to Piper's house until he pulled up to the dingy motel he'd seen when he spent all that time circling this town, looking for Piper's house. He had his father's credit card. Wasn't this the sort of thing that made his mother promise he'd always keep it, even though he tried to give it back? It was late. Phil drew the curtains tight and fell into bed to sleep long and hard.

*** 

*P*hil awoke to a grumbling stomach. It was pitch black in his room, except for the glowing 2:32 a.m. on the hotel alarm clock. He turned over a couple times in bed, lying on his stomach to try to squelch its annoying rumbling, but he was starving and he needed to eat. *Why hadn't he grabbed a burger or something before he checked in to the hotel?*

He didn't feel like driving around in the middle of the night like some sort of creep, so he grabbed some leftover food from his car—a half a bag of Doritos he'd bought at a gas station in South Dakota and some orange Gatorade.

He returned to his warm, hotel bed, turned on the television, and began rummaging through the crap programming that was only fit for insomniacs. He settled for an old episode of *M*A*S*H* crunching through the bag of chips.

*What was he doing here?* He wondered if he'd given himself a chance to properly think through what he was doing if he'd be in a different state right now, sleeping in a different bed. Maybe even thinking of a different girl. No, he could never go back to someone like Summer. Not now.

But Piper didn't want him. *Or did she?* He remembered the way she held onto him when he arrived. But when she'd turned him away earlier, it felt like she was saying for him to leave, but her eyes didn't dismiss him. The injured, prideful part of him wanted to get into his truck and head home. *Maybe she would realize her mistake if he did or would it make any difference at all?*

Something didn't sit quite right in his stomach with that thought—or was it the Doritos and Gatorade he'd inhaled? He had to try at least one more time.

Phil climbed out of the hotel bed and turned the hot water to run in the shower. He undressed and let the water stream from his head and down his body. It felt good. He turned the dial hotter and closed his eyes.

Her father had died. Of course she would be conflicted. Phil remembered the way she'd spoken of her father on that first night at her apartment. She had been so open and bright about him, like a child in her innocence. Losing her father would tear her apart. Even despite Phil's problems, he would be a wreck if his own father were gone. He'd give her the benefit of the doubt and hope that tomorrow she might feel differently.

He loved her. Now more than ever. Seeing her had brought everything back. He understood why he'd traveled all those miles, why he'd chosen her over Summer and his friends, why he wanted her with him. But he wanted her to be happy, happy to see him too. Maybe she was happier without him. He wasn't sure, but it didn't feel done. He had to find out for sure.

Phil let the water blast him in the face. Phil didn't want to come on too strong either; that approach had never worked with Piper. He would make himself available to her in the morning. *He would be there, nearby, without encroaching on her space, but how?*

He stepped out of the shower and toweled off. He wrapped the flimsy, white towel around his middle and stepped through the steam to the window, pushing the stiff curtains open. The world was still dark but, within that darkness, giant swirls of snow were falling. Maybe the snow could help him. *Shoveling had earned him Piper's address from her uncle, hadn't it?* Phil had a shovel in the back of his truck and he could go there and shovel, scraping just loudly enough for Piper to look out her window and see that he was still there. She would see that he hadn't given up on her and would be around to shovel, even if that was the only thing that could keep him around. Even if it was only for an hour or two. He would swallow his pride and wait for her to come to him. This thought seemed to sit a little better in his stomach.

## Chapter Twenty

*"I'll not put
The dibble in earth to set one slip of them."
-William Shakespeare*

𝒫iper couldn't sleep. After what seemed like hours of trying, she sat up in her childhood bed, tucked into the same quilt her mother had made and spread over her bed years before, and could just barely make out the contours of her bedroom from the streetlights outside. The room's striped walls were dotted with some old pictures of Piper, along with relics of high school—music medals and awards. The old, wooden chest that her father had built sat under the window with the cushion her mother sewed on top. She went to the window and opened the blinds. The night was a little brighter with the snow reflecting the moon back to her. She fixed her eyes on the street lamp and watched the occasional car drive by. Phil's car had been parked right below that street lamp. She wondered where he was. *Why had she sent him away when all she wanted was his arms around her, saying everything was going to be all right?*

Her mistake felt grave and permanent as things always did in the dark. Outside the snow fell, like glitter in the lamplight. She liked watching it, especially from the warmth of inside. She didn't understand why she was stepping out of her sleep pants and pulling on her jeans, and then her t-shirt, hoodie and socks. Piper crept down the stairs and found her coat and boots by the back door, next to Mopsa who was waiting to be let outside. They both escaped into the cold night.

The sidewalks were slick so Piper took each step carefully. She shivered in the cold but felt that now she could at last be free from the sadness pressing in on her inside the house. It felt good, just to be out. She walked, her lonely footprints in the snow leaving a trail behind her like breadcrumbs. It must not have been too late, as there were still cars driving past her. She'd watched them pass slowly. One every couple of minutes. She didn't have a specific destination in mind. She was just putting one foot in front of the other, searching for some clarity, hoping to figure out if sending Phil away was what she had really wanted.

She had gone three short blocks when a passing truck slowed beside her. She felt its presence but didn't look up. Piper tried to walk a little faster, but her footsteps were unsure. Maybe the person just needed directions. Maybe it was Phil, coming back to her as if she summoned him here. Maybe her brother had noticed she was gone and had come to look for her. She took a deep breath, exhaled a plume of cold air, and looked toward the truck when it skidded briefly on the ice and then stopped. The truck had snow piled on the top. Definitely not Phil or her brother. The window opened.

She looked around, no other cars. Nothing.

"Need a ride?" a man's voice called out. The voice was vaguely familiar, but she couldn't place it.

"No, thank you."

"You think it's safe out here?" the voice said, in a sort of flirty way. His face was dark within the shadows of his car, but Piper still couldn't get over the thought that she knew who this person was. *Maybe a neighbor or classmate from high school?* If not, she should be running away by now.

"Piper, you don't remember me?" His voice deepened, and the image of a face came to her. A face she'd dreamt about night after night in high school. In fact, she couldn't remember when her crush on him had begun.

*Maybe as early as elementary school?* He was always around—he had lived one street over from her. Piper thought their dads had even worked at the same company. They had ridden the same bus back in elementary school, but he never looked in her direction. As they got older, he always had some girlfriend, a cheerleader or student-body officer. Piper blushed in the dark. He'd never talked to her much in high school. There was the occasional "can I borrow a pencil" or "that quiz sucked" if they happened to be in a class together. She'd always smiled and nodded, always so agreeable and quiet and, here he was now, stopping in the middle of the night on the street of her childhood home. And he was asking her if she wanted a ride. Piper would have died for this moment a year ago.

"John Bersani," Piper said. "What are you doing here? I thought you'd be off at college becoming some kind of football god."

He scoffed, blended with a sharp outtake of breath. "Not likely. I had a knee injury in practice before school even began. That was the end. So I'm sitting out until next year, and I'll start over again. So much for the world is open to us. Remember that graduation speech? It seems so ironic when I think back on it, how naïve I was to believe it all. I came home and decided I'd start over again next year."

"It's not easy, is it?" Piper walked slowly closer to the car and leaned down toward the window. He was still good looking, in that jock sort of way. Dark, wavy hair cut short, dark brown eyes. He hadn't changed much at all since the last time she saw him at graduation. But he didn't sound like the jock she remembered him being. "I guess we all got our dose of the real world. Why are you out tonight, anyway?"

"My dad got me a job—night shift in the mail room at the company where he works. Where your dad worked. He retired about the time I started working there. Anyway,

I'm on my way home," John said. "I didn't think you stuck around home for school. Is it Christmas break already?"

"No," Piper said, a little sadly. "My father—he died this morning."

"I didn't know," he said, softly, like the snow landing on his arm, resting on the window opening. "I'm sorry."

Piper tried to smile and said, "More real world stuff, huh?"

"Yeah," he said, his eyes mirroring sympathy. "Listen, since you know I'm not some random guy, you want a ride?"

"So you haven't been drinking or anything, right?"

He shook his head and held up three fingers. "Scouts honor."

"You were a boy scout?" Piper asked, still unsure if she should get in the car or not.

"Back in sixth grade," he said.

Piper thought back and remembered his face clearly as he was in sixth grade, when they rode the bus together and she always knew where he was sitting or who he was sitting with. Back when he had been all bony shoulders and skinny legs. Before the football filled him in. Before all the girls.

*Today had been a horrible day*, she thought. *Why not? Isn't this what she had dreamed about for years, ever since those days on the bus in sixth grade? Being alone with John Bersani?* She couldn't let this opportunity slip past.

"Okay, thanks," she said, and carefully picked her way through the snow around the front of the car, opened the door, and slid in the passenger seat. Inside, the car was warm. Piper slipped off her gloves and stretched her hands in front of the heater vent.

John put the car in gear and carefully drove the snowy streets.

"How did he die?" he asked. He lowered the volume of the car stereo playing vintage Aerosmith on the radio for her response.

Piper turned to look out the window, not wanting him to see tears when they came. They wouldn't stop. "Cancer. But I just found out. My parents didn't want to distract me from my classes."

"When did you come back?"

"Yesterday," Piper said, then added. "And my father died today."

"Look," John said, as the car crawled to a stop in front of Piper's house. "I really am sorry about your dad. I remember seeing him mowing the lawn. And I know my dad thought a lot of him. Can I do anything for you?"

It seemed like an odd question. *What could he possibly do to help?* But it sounded thoughtful and it felt good to be the object of his thoughtfulness. Even if it was a year too late and the wrong guy. *Where was Phil in all of this?* Piper shook her head and smiled and shrugged. "You gave me a ride home."

He leaned his head back into the headrest, closed his eyes, and sighed as if about to speak—or fall asleep, Piper couldn't tell which for sure. After a while, he looked over to her.

"I always wondered about you," he said.

"Oh?" Piper sort of chuckled under her breath. "Not much to wonder about."

"Are you kidding?" he said. "The beautiful, mysterious musician? I used to hear music coming from your house when I'd ride my bike past or see you playing from the window. Sometimes I'd stop just a moment—tie my shoe or something—just so I could listen."

*Did he just say she was beautiful? He stopped in front of her house?* It seemed surreal. "I didn't think you even knew which house was mine," she admitted, then kind of wished she hadn't. She didn't want him to look at her like that, with pity. But that look didn't last long. He leaned back again and stared straight ahead.

"It's weird, you know, like if you knew somebody in third grade, they were always that same kid to you. Like they didn't grow up or something. I always kind of thought of you that way, the girl who rode the bus, always carrying a violin case, with curly pig tails." He turned toward her again. "And look, now you aren't—that same girl."

He brought his hand toward her face and cupped her chin, tilted her head up. It was the moment she'd dreamed of having a year ago, and now she wished the face on this boy wasn't his. When John brought her lips up to his, she didn't pull away. If there's one thing she'd realized since her father's death is that sometimes you don't get another chance. She didn't want to have regrets. She let the kiss happen, but knew straightaway that it didn't hold the same urgency the touching of two lips did when she was with Phil. Kissing John felt like "thanks for being here tonight" or two sixth graders hiding from the bus driver on the way home from school, but nothing more. She let him kiss her, though, for her sixth grade self.

The kiss didn't last long, and Piper thanked him for the ride home as she opened the car door and steadied her way through the snow to the back of the house.

***

*P*iper awoke to sun shining, feeling hopeful that maybe she could fix what she'd broken yesterday. She stretched as she lifted herself out of her bed and went to the window. What happened with John last night had seemed like a dream and today was her chance to make things right with Phil. Phil had said that he hadn't been with Summer. And if he had, now it seemed she was even. She felt guilty, though, thinking back on sitting in his car last night. The sun glistened off the white making the world feel sparkly and new. But things weren't shiny. Her father was gone, and nothing would ever be quite right again.

Piper heard the sound of footsteps down the hallway and slipped over, opening the door. Her mother was walking past in her night robe. Her walk was languid and her eyes red and swollen when they landed on her.

"Mom," Piper said, and reached out for her hand.

"I'm sorry if I woke you," she said, pausing at her door. "I didn't sleep well."

"I didn't either," Piper said, following her mother down the stairs to the kitchen. Dorcas darted past Piper on the staircase. "Mom, why don't you sit down for once and I'll get *you* something to eat?"

"No, I don't think—"

"Mom, I'm perfectly capable of toasting you a bagel."

"That's fine. I'll just wipe down the table," she said, reaching for the washcloth and turning on the water.

"You can't sit still, can you?" Piper said, as she pulled the bag of bagels from the refrigerator and began undoing the twisty tie.

"Honey, if I stop," Mom added, sadly, "I may never start again."

"Okay, Mom, wipe down the table if that's what you need to do."

Her mother had let Piper make the bagels, but she stayed busy in the meantime, setting out glasses of orange juice and pulling out some bananas. Setting a perfect table, just like something that could be straight out of an etiquette book. It was just how her mother coped.

They sat down to their bagels, but before they began eating, Piper said, "We are going to get through this."

Mom pursed her lips and nodded sadly. "I know, Piper. I'm so glad you're here."

"I wouldn't be anywhere else."

Midway through her bagel, Piper set it down and looked at her mom. "Mom, can I ask you something?"

"Sure, honey," she said. "What is it?"

"It's about yesterday. About what Dad said to me just before he died. It was strange—something about gifts and not being from you guys? He called me the strangest name. Perdita. Does that mean anything to you?"

Her mother shifted uncomfortably in her seat and took another bite of her bagel as if it was something she could do with her mouth instead of explaining. She chewed for a minute and swallowed.

"Piper, I think he wanted—" she said, and stopped. "He probably didn't know what he was saying."

"It seemed so important to him. Once he said it, he told me that he was ready to go. He really wanted me to know, but I couldn't make sense of it. Except that name, Perdita, I heard it recently."

Her knuckles white from her hands gripping each other, her mother said, "You know your father wasn't *quite right*."

"I know, Mom," Piper said, gently placing her hand over her mother's and rubbing, to keep them both warm. "I'm sorry. I don't mean to upset you. It just seemed like he was really trying to tell me something."

"Maybe he—"

Piper heard the sound of a shovel against pavement. Still, she waited to hear what her mother would say. Her mother rose from her seat and looked out the window.

"I wonder who that could be," her mother said.

Piper followed her mother to see the unmistakable stance of Phil shoveling the walk. She knew his snowboarding jacket and the way his body leaned against a shovel. The fact that he was there filled her with elation.

"Mom, that's Phil," she said. Piper wanted to get out there. She wouldn't risk not knowing where he was again. It felt like a second chance. "Can I go?"

"I'm not sure what happened yesterday," her mother said, as Piper was pulling on her boots. "But that boy has come a long way. At least bring him in for hot cocoa. I'll get some started."

"Okay," Piper said, as she wrapped her coat around her and then opened the door, letting in a pocket of snow-filled air. Piper blew out a big breath of air and walked carefully over the snow toward him.

She didn't stop and speak logically as she normally would. When he looked up and smiled a half smile as if he wasn't sure he should be there, Piper boldly put her arms around him and kissed him. She held onto him for so long as if daring the world to take him from her. She put her fingers against the warmth of his neck, just barely in the collar of his coat.

"I couldn't go back without seeing you one more time," he said, pressing her into a hug.

"I'm glad you're here," she kissed him again. "I want you here. I'm sorry for yesterday."

"I'm sorry too," Phil said. "For before."

"Come on in," Piper said. "My mom's making hot chocolate.

"But I just got started."

"It's time to warm up." She took his hand in hers and led him inside.

Mugs and a carafe of steaming cocoa were waiting on the kitchen table. Everything but Piper's plate had been cleared away. In the adjacent family room, her mother was brushing her hands free from wood debris near the fireplace as a small fire blazed.

"Mom," Piper said. "Come join us. Phil is someone I want you to know."

## Chapter Twenty-One

*"For I cannot be
Mine own, nor any thing to any, if
I be not thine."
-William Shakespeare*

𝓟hil felt complete, having Piper nearby. He was cold and he sipped the warm cup of chocolate while Piper and her mother told Phil about yesterday and how quickly her father had passed on after Piper arrived.

"He was waiting for you," Piper's mom said. "That was it."

Piper nodded, looking thoughtfully into her own mug. "I've heard of these things happening before but never to me, never to my family."

A guy with a sort of lanky, messy look came around the corner. Kind of like Shaggy from *Scooby-Doo*.

Piper stood. "Phil, this is my little brother Clint. Clint, this is Phil."

He was a nice enough guy, tall and just a little bit awkward, the way most high schoolers were. He came forward and shook Phil's hand. It all seemed so formal, but he was a good guy.

"I'll get you some cocoa," Piper said.

Clint sat down at the table, while Piper brought him over a mug.

Phil knew he was an outsider. To be here now, on this day, but for some reason he felt he belonged, as if he were part of this family.

They began discussing family matters, like when they would have the funeral and how it would all be arranged, who would do what. Phil stayed quiet and sipped from his mug. Phil felt the pressure of a cat near his ankle. He looked down to see Mopsa.

"Hey, I know you," he said, picking up the orange cat. "Come here." She curled into his lap while he petted her.

"You love Mopsa," Piper said, looking at him.

"I wondered where the cats were when I was waiting outside your apartment."

"I left so suddenly and I didn't know what to do with them. I couldn't just leave them there." Piper reached over and scratched under Mopsa's chin. "You didn't mind keeping me company on the car ride, right?"

"I could have used some company too," Phil said.

"I can't believe you came all this way—" she paused, then continued. "But I'm glad you did."

"So am I," Phil said. It was strange, sitting here with her family—it seemed so different from being at his house, where it was a rare day they all sat down at the table at the same time—but there was nowhere else he wanted to be.

They were making a checklist of things they needed to do and people to call when the doorbell rang.

"I'll get that," Piper's mother said, and padded slowly to the front door in her house slippers. They looked over as the gust of snow flew inside the house. There, framed in the front door was a dark-haired, middle-aged woman.

"May I help you?"

Silence. The woman just stood there, looking like she wasn't quite sure where she was. She wore a beige trench coat, tall brown riding boots, and a teal scarf. Her hair was tousled so that her bangs fringed into her eyes and the rest of her long hair angled toward her face in a haphazard sort of way. All Phil could see were her eyes, and they looked wide and scared. And skittish, as if she might turn and run instead of entering.

"Is there something I can do for you?" Piper's mother asked, again.

The woman nodded but still didn't speak.

Piper's mother opened the door wider and stepped back, motioning for the woman to enter. "Please, come in and warm yourself."

The woman paused and looked inside, like a cautious deer about to cross the street, then took slow careful steps into the living room and followed Piper's mother. She sat beside Piper's mother on the couch.

"Did you know my husband? Is that why you're here?"

The woman shook her head. When she did, the tips of her black hair brushed back and forth against her shoulders.

The woman gently took her hands and pulled the scarf down from her mouth. "Perdita," she said. The name was unmistakable even though her voice was hushed and cracked. Like she was weeping through years in each syllable.

Now it was Piper's mother who was speechless.

The woman repeated. "Perdita. Do you know where Perdita is? Is she here?" The woman looked anxiously around the house. Her eyes stopped on Piper.

Piper stood, the creak of the dining room chair against the wood floor the only sound.

"Mom?" Piper asked. Piper walked toward the woman and her mother as if in a trance. Her voice was more anxious now. "Mom, it's that *name* again. What is going on?"

The woman stood. "Are you—Perdita?"

Piper shook her head slowly. "No, I'm sorry, no," Piper said. "But I think I know who you are. MonaLee?"

The woman unabashedly draped herself around Piper. Piper's mother stood dumbfounded, along with Clint. Everyone watched motionless and silent, just soft mewing sobs came from the woman.

When the woman released her arms, Piper asked, "Why are you here? I mean, I know who you are. I found your letters."

"You got them?" The woman anxiously looked toward Piper's mother. That's when Piper's mother cupped her hands over her mouth, her eyes sorrowful.

"Mom," Piper said. "I need to know what's going on."

Piper's mother took a deep breath and nodded.

"It's time," she said. "This is when it all comes out. And now I have to do it alone." She paused, then continued. "Please, sit."

Phil joined them in the family room. That's when everything clicked. Phil knew why the letters came to Piper. She didn't accidentally find them in her viola case as Piper had assumed. They were put there for a reason, for Piper. The only thing Phil couldn't understand is why her mother would have sent them to her, especially the way her mother was acting now. Almost as if she's frightened for the truth to come out. *Maybe it had been Piper's father?*

Phil settled on the couch beside Piper. She clutched his hand as if he were some sort of lifeline.

"Piper," her mother said, as she took a deep breath. "Your father and I couldn't have children. We tried for years and years. We wanted a baby so much. I would have done anything to just have one baby."

Phil watched as Piper looked to Clint questioningly. Clint shook his head and shrugged as their mother went on.

"We tried to adopt, but it was taking so long. Finally, there was a baby. It was not through the state or other adoption channels. It was a friend of a friend of your father's who came to us and told us about the baby girl in need of a home. And we could have her right away. No loopholes, no waiting. But there was one stipulation: We could never tell her or anyone else that she was adopted. We had to sign papers promising that. I didn't care. I wanted you so much. I would have signed my soul away if they'd asked it." Slow tears were forming in her already swollen eyes.

Piper leaned forward, it seemed as if trying to get closer to her mother, hugging her from across the room. Phil couldn't help but watch MonaLee nervously fidgeting and tapping her slender fingers on her arms while folded, almost mimicking the way her fingers might have tapped against guitar strings long ago. Fingers that knew. MonaLee was nodding all the while and rocking back and forth. Probably some after effect from all those drugs she was kept on for years, he thought. Phil felt guilty for knowing about the adoption. He wished he didn't. He wished he were learning this now, with her. But maybe this was better. She'd be shocked and he could focus on comforting her. Phil reached his arm up and wrapped it tightly around her, as if holding her steady and firm in this precarious moment.

"I'm Perdita?" Piper asked. "From the letters?"

"What letters? How do you know about Perdita?" her mom asked.

"You sent them to me, Mom." Piper said. "In the viola case?"

Piper's mother shook her head and said, "I didn't."

MonaLee chimed in, quiet and shaky but forceful, "I did. I wrote the letters to you, Perdita, and got them to you."

Piper shook her head, refusing everything that was coming at her, "I can't—I can't process this right now. It's impossible. Mom, but how could you have never told me?"

"Honey," Piper's mother pleaded. "You have to understand. I couldn't. I didn't want to risk anything. I didn't know what could happen. Or if I could still lose you."

"But Mom, this changes everything," Piper said.

"No, it doesn't," her mother said, shaking her head.

"It changes who I am," Piper said, softly.

MonaLee spoke again, "It's not her fault. Please don't be upset. I didn't come here to turn your world upside down. I'm here because I needed to make sure you're okay. I wanted to see you. I've dreamed of you for years and knew in my heart that you were still alive, though I'd been told differently. And here you are, more beautiful and amazing than I could have imagined. She took good care of you, and I thank her for that." The two women exchanged soft looks.

MonaLee was shaking, as if still cold inside the warm house with a fire roaring nearby. The woman seemed nothing like the confident girl singing in the picture she'd seen on her laptop, as if her soul had atrophied along with the rest of her body.

Piper looked back to her mother, not quite done with the explanations. "What about Clint? Who's he?"

"After you were here, it's like something was lifted. And he came to us, naturally, after we had given up the possibility of having biological children."

Piper stood. "This is all too much. I need to be alone," she said, and was heading to the stairs when someone pounded on the front door.

Piper's mother went to the door, opening it a sliver. "Yes?"

"I'm looking for a woman," a deep voice said. "I have reason to believe she's here."

MonaLee cowered onto the couch when she heard him.

It was the Senator. Piper acted before she had time to think. She had to keep MonaLee safe from him and being in the clutches of that drug-bound existence. Piper ran and lunged toward MonaLee, pulling her out of the living room and back through the kitchen and out the back door.

"Phil, I need my mom's keys to her sewing studio," Piper whispered, after the door closed. "Please grab the key chain hanging from the hook by the back door? The one with the spool of thread."

Phil creaked open the door and fumbled around until he found the key chain. He heard Piper's mom still talking with the man, the Senator. He slipped back outside.

He passed the key to Piper who turned the frozen doorknob to the studio until the door opened. Piper locked the door behind them. It was cold inside. Several faceless mannequins were clustered in the left corner, one naked pale form exposed beside her two elegantly dressed friends. A desk with a sewing machine stood perpendicular to a wide table supporting several unwound spools of fabric on the other side of the open room. Piper turned on an electric fireplace near the desk. The flame glowed fake orange and yellow, but the heat that came from the box was comforting. It was probably the only source of heat in the small studio.

Piper pulled the curtains shut, saying to MonaLee, "You have to keep away from him."

"I knew this would happen," MonaLee said, her voice shaking. "I don't know where to go. I took one of his cars. It was the only way I could escape."

Phil sat on the chair to the desk and said, "He knows it's his car parked outside."

"I didn't know what else to do." MonaLee was still shaking, despite the warmth filling the room. Phil wondered if it was the reaction to her going without the drugs she'd been spoon-fed for the last twenty years or if she was frightened she'd have to go back to him.

"We can't let him find her. Should I call the police?" Piper asked.

"Yes, but I'm afraid it will be too late. He's here right now, and your mom doesn't know what we know," Phil said. MonaLee was standing stock-still by the door as if in a trance, like another mannequin.

Piper dialed 9-1-1 with the phone on her mother's desk. As she described what she considered to be a domestic-violence situation, the woman on the other end said someone would come shortly to check things out, but the calm voice spouting the information enraged Piper. She hung up with a quick thanks.

"Unless there's a gun or blood, it's not a priority," Piper said, shaking her head.

"He knows I'm here," MonaLee said, beginning to move again. She paced in front of the door. "I won't go back with him. I'd rather die. I'll kill myself."

"No, you can't. I never got to know you," Piper said. "And I want to."

There was a knock on the studio door. "Piper? What's going on?" It was Piper's mother. "Why are you out here? Where is—the woman?"

Phil looked out the window and said, "*He's* not with her."

Piper opened the door carefully. "Mom," she whispered, pulling her inside and shutting the door, locking it. "Don't allow that man in here. Did you tell him anything?"

"No," her mother said. "Just that there was a woman who showed up out of nowhere, that it seemed to be a day of random people showing up at our front door."

"Good," Piper said, as she put her arms around her mother. "Thank you."

"What's going on?" her mother asked. "Who is that man?"

"It's MonaLee's husband or captor, really," she said. "Mom, it's terrible. He's been drugging MonaLee and keeping her there like a prisoner. She can't go with him. We have to stop him!"

Phil looked out the window to the back door open again, this time the Senator and Clint were walking toward the studio. There was no other way out of the studio but the front door.

Another knock came to the door. Phil didn't think; he grabbed the undressed mannequin and pushed it against the wall, in a niche beside the antique hutch where rolls of colored fabric were stacked. He wordlessly led MonaLee over to where the mannequin had stood. Phil put a finger to his lips, letting her know not to speak. Piper grabbed the wide-brimmed hat from one of the mannequins and placed it on MonaLee's head at an angle, to hide her face.

"Just don't move and it will be fine," Piper whispered. "And let me do the talking."

Piper nodded to Phil to open the door. Piper's Mom stood by her desk.

With his hand on the knob, Phil looked back at MonaLee to make sure all was fine. Her skin was very pale. The bit of her that was exposed, her hands and a small portion of her jaw were almost as white as the mannequins posing beside her, probably from years and years locked inside that room with the sun just a memory. He opened the door. "Yes?"

Clint and the Senator stood just outside. Phil gestured them to enter.

## Chapter Twenty-Two

*"No longer shall you gaze on't, lest your fancy*
*May think anon, it moves."*
*-William Shakespeare*

𝒯he wide-brimmed hat covered most of her face. Maybe they could get away with this. Piper was glad to have Phil here. His idea could work. As she placed the hat on top of MonaLee's head, she looked into her eyes. Eyes that mirrored her own. This woman was her mother, yet Piper still didn't seem ready to accept it. Piper looked at her, so near her face, and could see the familiarity—her dark, dark hair and the small straight nose. Piper quickly took in the features that she'd looked at herself her whole life. It was strange to see them older and yet the same, sort of like looking into her future.

    Piper felt ashamed thinking of MonaLee like that, as if already replacing her mother with this woman she just met. She looked toward her mom of almost twenty years, concern knit over her worn-out face, and felt love. This woman was everything to Piper. She was the one who had spent hours making lunches for her, helping with homework, talking over friend problems, driving her to practices. Her features were nothing like Piper's, yet that was the face she equated with love. And now she knew what her mother had sacrificed for her. While Piper initially felt betrayed at what seemed to be a trick or dishonesty, it was all done in love. *And how could she be mad for being over-loved?*

    When Phil opened the door, Piper was ready.

"Why are you guys out here?" Clint asked. "And where is—"

"That woman?" Piper said, swishing her arm toward the door. "Who knows? It's not like we were actually going to buy any of that quack potion she was *selling*. I told her she was too late. No juice was going to make Dad's cancer turn around and even if it could have, she was too late. The nerve of her coming around here trying to make a buck off Dad's illness."

Clint looked perplexed. "But she…."

Piper took over. "… was so clueless. I mean, what kind of neighbor never comes by until Dad gets sick and then thinks she could get him to buy some green drink in her ridiculous, pyramid scheme. And anyway, who tries to make that kind of claim? That it can heal cancer? It's people like that who really piss me off. Take your green juice and shove it up…."

"Piper," her mother said. "You don't have to be so rude!"

"Are you kidding, Mom? You should have been *more* rude," Piper shot back.

The Senator stood there, looming over it all with his air of superiority, listening to it all.

"And who are you?" Piper continued, looking at the Senator. "Don't tell me you're selling something? Life insurance? Or maybe you have a magic, cancer-reversing bean? Have a life reversing bean in your pocket?"

"Piper!" her mother shouted. "That's enough!"

Yes, that was enough. Her mom was right. It wasn't like Piper, especially to talk to a stranger this way, but she felt she had a part to play in saving MonaLee's life.

"No," he said, coming toward her with his hand outstretched. "I'm not selling anything. I'm Senator Leo Stately. Of New Hampshire. I'm sorry to bother you now. I didn't know about your loss, and I'm sorry."

Piper backed up, refusing his hand, and nodded that she understood. Still, she couldn't believe how perfect his little speech sounded, as if he were reading it off some teleprompter with its perfectly placed pauses and sympathetic nuances.

But this man was her father. He was tallish and thin, black hair peppered with silver. Straight, white teeth and a strong chin. He looked dignified and professional. He was wearing a button-down shirt and khaki pants with a pair of loafers. Just what any politician might be wearing on a day off. He had a little scruff on his face, as if he'd not shaven this morning and hadn't had a chance to put on his "public" face. He was good looking in an older, professorial sort of way.

"I'm looking for a woman. In fact, the car she's driving is parked in front of your house. It's very important I find her. She's ill. Have you seen this woman?" He took a photo out of his wallet and brought it in close to Piper. It was an older photo of MonaLee, younger and vibrant and beautiful, not like the woman Piper hid under the wide-brimmed hat. "Was this the woman with the green juice?"

Piper shook her head. "No. But if this person is so sick, maybe you should go find the green-juice lady. It'll cure *anything.*"

The Senator stared at her as if not quite understanding her, almost like he knew this sort of sarcasm wasn't characteristic of Piper. "I'm sorry. I don't mean to waste your time." He was using an authoritative, deep voice that seemed used to getting whatever it wanted, but he wouldn't this time.

"I know who you are," Piper said, looking him square in the eyes. She shouldn't have said it. It meant she was admitting that she knew more than she should, that she knew about MonaLee, and was maybe even harboring her. But it was also a challenge.

"And I know who you are," he replied, in a softer tone. "Piper." He whispered her name tenderly, as though he were feeling something. Like love. Piper tried to push the idea that he was her father away. He was a monster. She knew that all too well. She wouldn't let the hush in his voice change what she knew.

"Don't pretend like you care about her," Piper said, her eyes fixed on him and unblinking. "I know what you've done. I know everything. And don't bother looking for her. She's gone now."

"But the car—it's out front," he said, with a little less certainty.

"You don't understand what I'm saying," Piper said, and moved to the other side of the studio, away from the mannequins and toward her mother. "She's *gone*. But she's safe now, from you."

"Gone? Where? But I have to get to her. It's urgent."

"Yeah, right," Piper said. "It's *urgent*. Here, why don't you take MonaLee back to the dungeon? What did you think was going to happen here?" It surprised Piper how aggressively she was speaking to the man who could have been her father in a different sort of world. The room and everyone else in it seemed to melt away, and it was just Piper and the Senator. "You can't drug someone so they can't get out of bed for years and then think she will be just fine. So are you happy now? Isn't that what you wanted all along was for her to be gone? So you could sweep away the one, glaring skeleton in your closet? Your life's big mistake!"

He crumpled onto the bench by the door and buried his head in his hands. "You don't understand." He shook his head and the room was silent. He began digging into his pockets and pulled out a rattling, plastic cylinder. "Look, it's her medicine. She needs this." He held the bottle out to Piper, his eyes earnest and moist.

Piper just watched him, her hands shaking, yet she was beginning to feel something. *Could it be compassion for this monster who ruined so many lives in his path?* If she weren't so angry, Piper could perhaps feel sorry for seeing this grown man with tears pooling.

After some time, she took the cylinder, looked at the name on it, and threw it away in the trash can near the desk. "So, what? You have a doctor prescribe her drugs. You can pay off anybody. I know what you're capable of."

The Senator stood and held up his chin. "Please trust me that I can help her. You think you understand, but you don't. She's ill. How could you possibly know anything about her? About me?" He then turned to Piper's mother, standing behind her desk and staring wide-eyed toward him. His voice shifted to stern. "She wasn't to be told anything."

"I didn't know anything," her mother said. "I have no idea where she heard all of this."

He shook his head again, flustered, and muttered, "I'm sorry. But it's not uncommon for kids to be adopted secretively. This has been happening since the beginning of time."

At those words, Piper felt her own face drop, her tough-girl façade begin to melt away and turned into an abandoned, little girl. She tried to hold in a sob, but it came too quickly. It was something she had never felt until now, until she saw the person who had ripped her away from her mother as a baby and sent her far away, like some horrific fairytale. But it had really happened to her. Even at her age, it was easy to feel disposable and unwanted. She took a deep breath and tried to resume her fighting stance.

He then put his arms up, as if giving up and implying he lost. "Okay. I'll tell you everything if you'll listen. You should be allowed to know, after all, this is where you came from," he said, implying he himself was her father. "Do you want to know?"

A cry sounded from MonaLee just before she dropped down to the ground, straight-legged, as if she were pushed over by a breeze. She lay on her side, her hands curled into tight claws and her body jerking on the floor.

Phil was nearest to MonaLee and he rushed over, followed by Piper, who both kneeled to her. They didn't know what to do.

The Senator followed with a pillow from the bench, pushing the closest mannequin away from MonaLee to give her more room. He tucked a large, green pillow under MonaLee's shaking head and turned her face to the side and some saliva, blood, and vomit dribbled out of her mouth onto the tile.

"We need to call an ambulance!" Piper cried out.

"It's okay," the Senator said, calmly. "She's just bitten her tongue. She's going to be okay. See, the convulsions are slowing down."

MonaLee stilled and opened her eyes. She looked disoriented and squinted, as if she had no idea where she was or who anyone was.

"She needs that medicine. Can you get it from the trash can?" the Senator asked Piper.

She looked at him, resolutely, and shook her head. Nobody moved. Finally, he stood up to get it himself.

"And water," the Senator said, as he rushed across the room. "She needs a glass of water."

"I'll get her water," Clint said, and hurried out the door, letting a draft of freezing air peppered with snowflakes into the studio before whipping the door shut behind him.

Piper jumped up. "No! I will not let you put any of those pills in her body." She ran to the trash and tried to snatch the bottle out before he could. She gripped it in her white-knuckled hand, and he backed up, putting both his hands in the air, in surrender.

MonaLee cried and tried to push herself off the floor into a seated position but collapsed again. The Senator made his way back to MonaLee and crouched onto the floor, with Piper not far behind.

"No," Piper said. "Don't touch her!"

"I'm trying to help," he said. The Senator backed away and spoke again, soft like trying to calm a scared animal into submission. "Please."

"You can't help her," she said, holding the rattling bottle with both hands. "I know what you've done."

"Please. I don't want to see her hurt." He shook his head and stood, to face Piper. "I felt I had no other option but to keep her safely under my roof."

"Are you kidding? She wasn't safe! She was your prisoner!" Piper shouted, then she softened her voice. "Why couldn't you just love her? That's all she wanted from you. And to have someone to love."

"It wasn't so simple," he said, and brought over a single chair and set it before MonaLee, then gestured to Piper. "She needs this medicine now, before—

"No," Piper bent over and put her arms around MonaLee to help her sit on the chair. "And it was simple. You stole her freedom and her baby." Piper's voice cracked when she realized that baby—MonaLee's baby—was herself. That she was this baby who was torn away from its mother.

Piper also realized that MonaLee's frail body was still heavier than she could maneuver. The Senator stepped over to help nudge her into the chair. MonaLee's eyes were following Piper, but then shifted, seemingly registering nothing but confusion.

Clint opened the door and walked toward MonaLee with a glass half filled with water. He stopped and looked toward Piper and the Senator. Piper stepped forward with her hand outstretched, daring the Senator to try to take charge again. "Thank you, Clint."

"Please listen to what I have to say," the Senator continued, and pleaded with his eyes. "MonaLee has suffered for a very long time from schizophrenia and epilepsy. When we first met, I knew about the seizures. She'd been on medication for years before then. It started getting worse, though, and she told me that sometimes voices in her head would tell her to do things. Usually this would happen just after a seizure. Or tell her that people wanted to do things to her, making her paranoid."

Piper held the glass out to MonaLee but she stared straight ahead. Piper turned back to the Senator, with a skeptical look in her eyes, but he had her attention. She didn't speak, just waited for him to continue.

"When she was pregnant, she had one of her seizures. They would often start with a migraine headache and she would lie down. Then she would awaken and come at me, usually crying and yelling. Sometimes she would get violent, and I'd have to hold her down until it ended. She probably shouldn't have gotten pregnant, but I didn't realize just how serious it was until after it was too late."

Piper looked toward Phil, who was standing near Clint by the door, to gauge if *he* believed this guy. His eyes looked just as unsure as she herself felt. Piper then looked to her mother who was seated near her desk, her eyes wide in disbelief.

"Once, late in the pregnancy, I found her in the kitchen with a chopping knife aimed at her stomach. I held her back, but she cried and said that her baby wasn't mine. That the baby belonged to someone else. She said she'd made a pact with the devil and that he was her lover. It was all so fantastical that I just tried to keep her from hurting herself. But I knew when the baby came, she wouldn't be able to care for it. I was afraid that if we kept the baby around—you, Perdita—she would try to be the mother she could have been, but that she might hurt you. I couldn't take that chance, so I did what I had to do.

"I found a family, a loving set of parents who I knew would give you the life you deserved. It was very difficult, and I didn't take the decision lightly. I never forgot about you. I checked in all the time with your... father."

"But why," Piper asked, tears in her eyes. "Why couldn't I know?"

The Senator shook his head slowly.

"I didn't want to make things harder for you. I didn't want you to feel torn in your loyalties. I wanted you to be a happy, normal, well-adjusted kid. Well, and I lead a public life. So did MonaLee in her past. I didn't want this getting out. I didn't want the media to have a frenzy about the pop star who went crazy or the politician who married her."

"But MonaLee," Piper said, looking to her, then back to the Senator. "Why did you tell her I had died?"

"I never said that," he said. "But she has this inner voice that tells her things—about everyone around her and who's doing things to her, telling her to hurt them before they can hurt her. Nothing I say makes a difference. She needs to get back on her medication."

MonaLee was rocking slowly back and forth on the chair, with her eyes glazed over. She hadn't even looked over when Piper said her name.

Piper looked to Phil, then back to the Senator. "How do I know it's true?"

The Senator began digging into his pocket and pulled out a card. He leaned over and handed the card to Piper.

"Here, this is the name of her physician. Dr. Reed. He has been caring for her for many years in my home. She's been stabilized, taking the seizure medicine. And other drugs for her schizophrenia. I hate that she can't be the vibrant, talented woman I once knew. But, when I married, I married the woman I loved and I couldn't leave her. I still keep a seed of hope in my heart that one day, she will be able to heal so I can have back the woman I fell in love with. So I can have a marriage—and maybe, now that you know, you could be a part—"

The letters! Piper tried to think back on the letters. *Could they have been the result of the hallucinations of a very sick woman? Could it have all been paranoia?*

MonaLee stood suddenly, springing out of her chair and darted toward the table. She grabbed a pair of sewing scissors lying beside a half-cut fabric pattern, and held the blade inside her fist overhead, aimed at the Senator. The Senator tried to reach for the scissors, which was already dripping blood from MonaLee's hand. Phil and Clint stood unsure what to do, their hands ready. The Senator tried to grab MonaLee's arm, but only managed to grab her around the waist.

Piper turned around to see cold fire in MonaLee's eyes, aimed right at her.

"I remember you! You're Satan's Child," MonaLee screeched, and thrust the scissor's blade at Piper's face. Piper wasn't sure how her mother had gotten to her so fast, but as the blade was coming down, her mother pushed Piper away from the scissor's path. Piper felt the sharp pain of steel slicing through the arm of her sweater.

The Senator was beside Phil, holding down MonaLee's arm, wrenching the scissors out of her grasp. Piper's mother was at Piper's side, with some fabric from the table, pressing it on her arm.

"I'm so sorry. This is what I worried about," the Senator said, in between heavy breaths, straining to keep MonaLee contained. He shook his head, and his eyes held true sorrow. "I brought her medication."

Clint went to the telephone on the desk and dialed 9-1-1. As the Senator forced the medication into MonaLee's mouth, she struggled against him but finally coughed the pills down with water.

Piper heard a banging outside. Phil turned from the window.

"The paramedics are here," he said. "I'm glad we called before." He swung the door open and yelled, "Back here! We're in here!"

Piper watched as if life were in mute and slow motion while the paramedics talked briefly to the Senator, then put something for MonaLee to breathe over her mouth and strapped her to a gurney. It wasn't until MonaLee was being carried out of the door that an EMT came over to her. Her mother was still pressing the wadded fabric onto Piper's arm and Phil had been by her side, holding her. Piper had been cocooned in love the whole time as she watched the paramedics in a daze.

It wasn't until the paramedic knelt down over them that Piper looked down.

"Mom," Piper said, reaching out to her mother's arm. "You're bleeding too."

## Chapter Twenty-Three

*"You gods, look down,
And from your sacred vials pour your graces
Upon my daughter's head!"*
-William Shakespeare

*P*iper and her mom got five stitches between the two of them. Not bad considering how much blood had swamped their clothes and the bolt of fabric they had shared, balling it up and pressing onto their wounds on the car-ride to the hospital. Piper looked down at the scarlet blood blotting continent-like shapes between their two worlds, focusing her attention away from the pain coursing its way down her arm.

The paramedic had looked at Piper and her mother before leaving with MonaLee in the ambulance and suggested Phil or Clint drive them to the ER. He told them they would be okay if they went straight there.

The waiting room gave off a sterile, stuffy scent. The chairs were filled with sniffling children and anxious parents. She and her mother explained they needed to see a doctor and the blonde girl with glasses, at the check-in desk, handed them each a clipboard with forms to fill out. They found a cluster of empty chairs together.

Piper gripped a pen in her hand ready to fill out the standard papers, but thought a little bit about the common sort of question that asked her to simply jot down her name. Which now required a lot of introspection. Yes, Piper was her name. *But where inside Piper was Perdita, the baby she had been to the mother who despite her illness had never stopped thinking of her and writing letters to her?* As if that

Perdita actually existed somewhere. Piper swallowed a lump in her throat and looked over to her mom and wondered how she was filling out her own forms, about being married or not. About her health insurance that was tied to Piper's dad who was no longer there. "Nothing's changed, you know," Piper said. "In light of all this *new* information."

She nodded with sadness in her eyes. "You understand, don't you? Why I couldn't tell you?"

Piper nodded and pressed her hand over her mother's. "I know. I can see now."

Her mom released a soft sigh. They both watched as a young mom led a small girl through the metal doors. There was something about the all-encompassing love a mother has for her child, like a blanket always warm and ready.

Piper began writing her name on the form. P-i-p-e-r. She had been born a baby named Perdita, who couldn't be loved the way she should. So she became Piper and fit into a life where she belonged. Things would have been different had the Senator made another choice. She couldn't blame him for what he had done. It was ultimately the best thing for her. She knew that now. But wow, did this rock her safe, little world!

Next came the slot for her address. She wrote her childhood address in the line, but did so slowly and carefully, wondering where home would have been had MonaLee not been sick.

She ran her eyes over all the vast questions that seemed to carry more weight and significance now that she knew the ailments of her mom—sitting beside her—probably had no direct bearing on her own body. And it made her mind reel to think of the psychological issues MonaLee had. *Could they, would they be genetic? Could she have schizophrenia, too?* Piper sat staring at the tiny letters on the pages, flipping through them anxiously, while the world seemed to spin around her in its crazy path. She didn't want to try to fill out forms that she had always known how to answer, but suddenly didn't.

Her legs felt jittery and she felt anxious sitting there. "I can't," she said, shaking her head, all the questions still lingering in her periphery. "I don't know how to fill this out."

Phil put down the magazine he had been leafing through, his warm leg pressed against hers, and grabbed the clipboard.

"Piper," he said, pushing the clipboard behind his back and turning to face her. "You've been through a lot. I know you have. But deep down, you've always known, and you still do, who the girl is sitting before me." He cupped his hands gently under her chin. "You're the most amazing, kind, beautiful person I've ever met. It doesn't matter who carried you, or where you started, but where you are now. This doesn't change who you are."

"Thank you," she whispered, and fell into him for a hug, her mouth to his ear. "For being here with me. Through all this."

"I wouldn't be anywhere else."

The rest of their time at the ER was spent in small talk with a nurse, some more waiting, and a couple minutes being sewn back together again with a scrub-wearing doctor. Back at home, Phil turned all-protective on her upon returning, insisting Piper stay in bed and rest. He sat in the chair beside her bed.

"I'm fine," Piper said, over and over, but she admitted she hadn't slept enough in the past several days and wouldn't mind a little nap. She took a series of naps interspersed with her mother drifting in and out of her room, asking her little details about the funeral that she and Clint were trying to finalize. Phil was always nearby.

After a while, Piper opened her eyes to the muffled sound of Phil and her mother whispering. She understood her mother saying, "He wants to see her," and Phil responding with some mumbled words, Piper barely making out "needs her rest," before she let out a loud breath and struggled to a sitting position in bed.

"Honey, how are you feeling?" her mother said, then patted her gently on the shoulder.

"Better." Piper reached for the glass of water sitting on the nightstand. It was cool and still clanked with ice, as though it had been refreshed while she slept. She chewed on a small piece of ice—an old habit she never could quit—and asked, "How are you, Mom? Shouldn't you be resting?"

"Every time I try, my mind ends up going a mile a minute. I've got a funeral to plan and so much to think about." She fussed a little over Piper's covers, making sure they were straight and tightly spread over her. "Thank goodness for Phil. At least you're taken care of."

Piper smiled over at Phil, who kept watch like a sentinel. He had a book in his hand as he sat nearby the bed.

"Are you up for a visitor?" he said, smiling. "The Senator?"

She nodded and brushed her hair down, in an attempt to look presentable.

When the Senator came in, his smile was so genuine. His eyes lit up to see her. Phil set down the book, stood and offered the Senator his seat.

"Thank you," the Senator said, placing his hand on Phil's shoulder with a nod of thanks.

Phil picked up the water cup. "I'll go refresh your cup and be back in a minute."

The Senator looked down into his hands where they were clasped together. "MonaLee's going to be okay. She has round-the-clock care, but it's important she stays on her meds."

Piper nodded, her mouth drawn down. "I'm sad for her. It's not fair to have to live a life like that, always medicated, never free." Piper smoothed down the hem of her grandmother's quilt in the same way her mother had. It felt stable and reassuring. "But I understand. Now. I'm sorry I accused you."

"How would you know?" he said. "She really believes that I am trying to harm her."

Piper didn't respond right away, looked him bold in the face. "But how could you give me up so easily? Couldn't *you* have kept me?"

He shook his head, slowly, his eyes moistening. "I loved you so much. I still do. It might not seem like it, but I didn't want you raised by nannies and that's what I'd have had to do. I was always so busy. I'm always traveling, always away late even when I'm in town. And I worried that keeping MonaLee from you would be like torture to her. We couldn't give you the home you needed. My intentions were good."

The door slid open and Piper's mother entered silently with a small vase of flowers, some white stargazer lilies. She placed them on the nightstand. The flowers' sweet scent began to fill the room. Her mom stooped to pick up some things on her floor and put them up.

"I kept in contact with your father. Often. I never stopped thinking about you. I never forgot your birthdays. I always sent you something. And I visited you, although you didn't know."

"No," Piper said, confused. "I never got anything from you."

"You did," Piper's mom said, framed in the door as she had been walking out. She turned back toward Piper. "Those gifts. Don't you remember the carousel music box and the velvet coat with the gold buttons?"

"I loved that coat," Piper said, smiling remembering it. "I always wanted to wear it; I just didn't have anywhere special enough to wear it to."

"Your dad and I could never afford gifts like that," her mother said. "But when they were delivered to our home, we wanted you to have them."

"I wish I could have seen you in that coat," he said, a bright smile, raw and emotional, on his lips. "I hand-picked it from a boutique while I was in Paris. I imagined the blue matching your eyes. Your father sent me photos so I knew you had MonaLee's blue eyes."

Her mother said to the Senator, "It did match her eyes, quite perfectly, and the coat was beautiful on her."

Piper remembered the coat, every pleat and cuff. Each button could have been the centerpiece of its own necklace. The coat still hung in her closet just several feet away. She received it on her seventh birthday. Her mother had to peel it off her just so she could eat cake and ice cream. She couldn't get any ice cream stains on that *lovely velvet.* Even though it didn't really matter; she never got to wear it anywhere.

It was then that Piper thought about the stark comparison her little family home, warm and cozy, probably had to the grand estate where she would have grown up had she grown up with her biological parents. She lived with a quiet family as opposed to a life in the spotlight. Still, she was glad of her humble upbringing and wouldn't have wanted anything different. She had been here for a reason with two parents who couldn't have loved her more, in a quiet town. This was all she needed. She looked around her room and thought how everything that was right in the world was hers in this place, right here in the middle of nowhere Minnesota.

As she scanned the room, she focused on the wall-shelf where her carousel music box still sat. Birthday nine. She'd loved that so much and had wound it up every night before bed. It played Fur Elise. The slow movement of its beautiful carved animals, circling round and round, and the tinkling melody lulled her to sleep many nights. Maybe unknowingly, she felt the reach of her father through that lullaby.

He was so different from the man she'd always thought of as her father. Her Dad was simple, and normal, and just so always there. The man before her now was none of those things. She didn't know if she could ever love him the way she did her Dad, or if he even wanted that from her.

"I've always wanted to be a part of your life," the Senator said. "I was hoping someday to hear you play the viola, the one I sent."

"Of course," Piper said, shaking her head that she hadn't figured it out before. She looked over to the leather case settled in the corner of her room. "*You* sent the viola. Of course, it came from you."

"I was in Europe this summer and spent some time having a master luthier get the viola up to par," he said. "I wanted to give you something so you wouldn't abandon your gift."

"You knew about that?"

"I knew everything about you," he said. "One of the stipulations for the adoption was your parents had to send me monthly updates with pictures of you, your artwork and report cards, even videos. I've seen every one of your concerts and solos. I even attended one. I sat in the back, inconspicuously of course. When your dad told me what had happened with the audition and how you quit, it killed me to know you were throwing away your talent."

"I had to stop playing," she said, sick that her failure was spread out in places she never knew until now. "But I have played the viola you sent. I love it."

"Maybe someday," he said. He had his fingers steepled together and held them under by his nose, as if thinking. He looked vulnerable, almost pleading, and it seemed so wrong to deny him an opportunity.

"Honey," Piper's mother said. Piper hadn't even realized she was still standing there in the doorway. "I did want to ask you if you might play at the funeral tomorrow. Daddy would have wanted it so much, to see you play again."

The Senator nodded to Piper's mother, what seemed like an unspoken thank you between them.

Phil walked around the corner and said, "Don't use the excuse that you can't. I've heard you play, and you can."

"But my arm—," Piper said. She lifted it to see how it felt to move it. "At least the cut is on my upper arm, and it shouldn't impact my playing. I'll try. For Dad."

As her mother came to her and held her in an embrace, Piper's eyes fell on the white lilies sitting in the vase. A card was attached. When she looked to Phil, assuming the flowers were from him, she noticed his eyes locked on the flowers as well.

"Mom?" Piper said as she pulled out of the hug. "Where did these flowers come from?"

"They arrived a little while ago," she said. "They were sent to you. There's a card."

Piper leaned over with her good arm and pulled the little card from its small envelope, tucked into some foliage. The white petals curled open, like an offering. The card read:

*I wish I had known you and your family better. I hope it's okay if I attend the funeral with my father. My sincere sympathy, John Bersani.*

Piper froze as she read the words printed on the card with a white dove in the corner. She looked up to see both her mother and Phil waiting expectantly.

"It's from an old friend, from school," she said, and tucked the card back into the envelope. "You know, John

Bersani, whose father worked with Dad. They're coming to the funeral."

The Senator continued, looking at both Piper and her mother, "If it's all right with you, I'd be honored to pay my respects at the funeral as well."

Her mother nodded. "Yes, we'd like that."

The Senator stood. "I wish I could have been a bigger part of your life. But one thing I did right was give you the right family. You turned out strong and beautiful just as I dreamed you would. MonaLee wanted that, too."

The Senator turned and walked out. Phil took his chair beside the bed again. Her mother squeezed her hand. It was unspoken, but Piper knew her mother was proud of her too, no matter where she came from and who she turned out to be.

"I'll leave you two."

Phil grabbed the book from the table and held it up to her. It was Jane Eyre. He must have taken it from her bookshelf.

"Maybe you could relax, if I read aloud to you."

"You just won't give up until I'm strapped onto a snowboard, will you?" Piper laughed, remembering back to her original promise. She leaned back into her pillow and closed her eyes as Phil began reading.

"There was not a possibility of taking a walk that day."

## Chapter Twenty-Four

*"... there lies such secrets in this fardel and box, which none must know but the king, and which he shall know within this hour..."*
*-William Shakespeare*

$\mathcal{P}$hil stood outside the bedroom door, listening to the deep voice and quivering sadness of the viola playing the song Piper'd chosen—an old country song Piper said she remembered her father singing in the car when she was a little girl. Phil couldn't believe how strong she was—focusing on practicing when so many emotions must have been sifting through her mind. He loved the beauty of her music, and of her. He hoped he wouldn't stop feeling this way, but knew when the backdrop was his messy apartment filled with his rowdy friends, his love wouldn't seem quite so pure.

Phil needed to get back to work. He wondered if he still had a job. He had called and told his boss he'd be gone for a little while but didn't know what to expect when he returned. He had planned to leave tomorrow, after the funeral. Piper would be staying through Christmas, and he was returning alone. But it had been worth it. He needed to be with Piper; he was sure she felt the same.

He knew she wanted him there, especially when Piper ran into a guy she knew from high school at the funeral the next morning. This guy, John, watched her a little too closely and lingered a little too long. And he looked at her, with a little too much *concern*. It wasn't until Piper thread her arm through Phil's and introduced him as her boyfriend that he seemed to get the picture. Then he moved right along.

Piper played beautifully, as Phil knew she would. He heard little sniffles peppered from all around the United Church of God's pews, all the way up to the balcony in the back. The church was covered in flowers and their scent filled the place. Her father was very well liked in the community, as was apparent with all the flower arrangements set around the casket and the many people who showed up for the service. The minister said all the things ministers usually said, all those lines from the Bible, and it was done.

Phil decided to hang back and make sure the caterer arrived for the small luncheon. He saw the Senator standing around, looking about unsure as he did, and said he could help him get things ready for when the family returned from the cemetery.

"Thanks, uh, you're Piper's boyfriend?" he said. "I guess we were never properly introduced. Leo."

The Senator with his professional arm outstretched for shaking reminded him a lot of his own father back in California. Phil shook his hand, warily.

"Leo, I'm Phil. You know, it's sort of weird to know so much about you, when we haven't even exchanged names. But it's cool. You seem to care about Piper. And I care about Piper, so we have that in common."

The Senator nodded.

The smell of coffee filled the air. Phil looked around the hall at the people in white aprons setting out food onto the serving table and others laying table-sheets on the tables.

"It looks like the caterers are on top of everything."

The Senator bounced his finger in the air toward Phil. "You know, you remind me of an old friend of mine. Are you from around here, Phil?"

"Nah," he said, and shrugged in his carefree surfer attitude, then sat down at one of the tables. "Cali."

"California?" the Senator said, and sat across from Phil. "I had a prep-school friend back in New Hampshire who lives in California. Well, did last time I heard from him. I haven't seen him for years."

"Huh," Phil said, a little intrigued. "Must have been hard. Going to a stuffy, boarding school."

"It wasn't so bad," but he paused. "Actually, looking back on it. I wish I had been home, with my parents. Why couldn't it all have waited? The sculpting me into who my father wanted me to be."

When he looked back at Phil, his eyes were shiny and he smiled in that sort of way that looked like a frown, but the smile was for someone else. This was something Phil understood. The pressure from his family to be just the right fit into the mold his father expected. But his father hadn't sent him off to some boarding school and let teachers raise him.

Phil knew, as he was leaning in to hug the old man, that no two people in the world could have been more different—and more alike.

The Senator clung to Phil in a desperate way that reminded Phil of a child searching through the years for childhood love. The way a child hugs his parents with abandon. Not a care in the world for the people who butter his toast and put away his crayons.

Phil felt himself gravitating to this misunderstood man. This man who had tried to keep living his life despite so many problems. Who wouldn't give up on love, no matter what it meant.

After a while, Piper appeared by Phil's side. She stood there, hands clasped before her in her simple, dark blue dress. Her eyes were tender. He pulled her into his arms. He wanted to tell Piper how he could love every part of her—the mysterious Senator, the ill biological mother,

her humble mother, and the man she loved so much whose life they were celebrating today. He wanted to be a part of her complete, but outrageous life. But right now wasn't for Phil. Now the time was for her and for grieving her dad. Phil tightened his grip around her, kissed her on the forehead, and kept near her throughout the rest of the day, to keep her standing through the difficult moments ahead.

## Chapter Twenty-Five

*"The self-same sun that shines upon his court
Hides not his visage from our cottage, but
Looks on all alike."*
-William Shakespeare

**Izzie
20 Years Later**

*C*old, hard snowflakes pecked against the orange, plastic shield Izzie had lowered over her and her mom as they rode the lift up the mountain. The heated, lift seat penetrated through several layers of clothes.

"There were no fancy lifts like this when I worked here," Izzie's mom told her. "But that was a long time ago."

"Wow, mom," Izzie said. "Wasn't that before there were iPods and computers and televisions."

"Very funny, Izzie," her mom said, and gave her that purse-lipped smile and shook her head. "I'm not that old."

"What did you use to listen to music with when you were twelve?" Izzie asked, scrolling on her iPod touch.

"I had headphones, just they were a lot bigger and if you wanted to listen to something recorded, you had to put a tape into it."

"Wow," Izzie said. "Your life sounds hard."

"Not really," her mom said. "I had a good life."

*Izzie had to remember to go easy on her mom. Her mom began adjusting her gloves under her coat sleeves to make sure no skin was exposed. Again. Her mom was always so protective. Too protective. But today was a day for them. They were up on the mountain alone, for the first time since her dad died. Her mom was still so sad about it all the time, but they were celebrating him by doing what he loved: snowboarding. Izzie remembered the way her dad would lift her onto the lift, when she was not even in kindergarten. She loved being on the slopes with her dad and liked it even better when he looked at her all proud, brushing the snow off her teeny little snowboard. He'd put his arm around her, to secure her onto the lift, protecting her. The world was small then, and perfect. Her mom had learned how to snowboard, too. It had been so important to her mom that she learned and they had always told her stories about how her mom didn't want to do it, but ended up loving it. They took ski trips as a family each winter, to get Dad away from working so long every day. He took over Grandpa's company and was always so busy going to meetings and making important decisions and stuff.*

*Izzie remembers, on one of their last trips from California, she had awoken in the middle of the night and her parents were driving. They loved road trips, even though Izzie wanted to fly. And they spoke through the dark, their faces flashed with lights from the cars driving by on the freeway. They whispered about when they met. About flying down a ski hill riding a snowboard like a sled because her mom had been too afraid to snowboard for real. How her dad had even read Jane Eyre to try to win her mom. It was sweet—and weird—to hear about them falling in love. But Izzie remembered shifting her pillow and blanket in the back, feeling so comfortable in the back of the car knowing how much they loved each other. She was safe in this comfortable, little world.*

*It was a year since her dad's death. He was helicopter snowboarding, and he and some other guys got stuck in an avalanche. Her mom was looking out over the vast mountains and Izzie knew why. She could feel her dad with her, and her mom probably felt it too. Like he was watching them from every eye of those silvery, white birch trees lining the lift's path. Her mom took a deep breath, wove her arm through Izzie's and stared ahead.*

*"The lifts didn't go this way when your dad and I worked here," her mom said, in a whisper. "Some big company bought this ski resort, and then another owner changed it, too. All this terrain was backcountry when we worked here. It's hard to tell where the old lifts had been." She finished with a crack in her voice, just a little, as if not talking to Izzie.*

*"Mom," Izzie said, and leaned her head onto her mom's shoulder. "Don't be sad. Daddy wouldn't have wanted it."*

*Izzie knew her mom was maybe crying inside the dark shade of the goggles she was wearing. She had cried a lot at first, but had gotten better since Daddy was gone. But it was still hard. For both of them. She hated seeing her mom cry and that made her upset.*

*Her mom said she looked like Dad. In almost every way, except the eyes. Izzie's eyes were the identical ice blue of her mom's and Nana, her mom's biological mother who had always been sick. Izzie's mom talked about her and Izzie had met her a couple times, but they didn't go visit a lot because she had to live in a special hospital and Nana scared her with the weird things she said when they did visit. Nana died a couple years ago. Izzie never really knew her much, though. Her mom had said she was happy in a way, because she was set free from her broken body.*

*And her grandpa was free, too. Finally. Her mom told her how they used to call Grandpa "the Senator." Well, he was a senator for a lot of years. But her mom never called him Dad. That was sort of weird. She had a different dad who had died years before. The grandpa who brought her mom her first viola. Izzie would never forget that story. Her mom talked about it every time she made Izzie practice her cello. Izzie got kind of tired hearing about it. But still, it was kinda sweet. Izzie felt sad that she never got to meet that grandpa. He sounded so nice. Grandma still talked about him all the time, always with a sad, wet look in her eyes. Grandma was waiting down at the lodge with a book in front of the fire. She didn't like to ski, but liked going with them on most of their trips.*

*"That," her mom said, pointing to an old building that smelled like hamburgers. "It's the same restaurant I remember."*

*"Mom," Izzie said, "Listen, it's that song you like. The reggae one."*

*"One Love," her mom sang lowly along with Bob Marley as it pumped out from the outside speaker. "Let's get together and feel all right."*

*Her mom looked to her, shaking her head and softly laughing. "I can't believe it. Some things never change. After all this time, they are still playing Bob Marley."*

*"Why? You still listen to it."*

*"It reminds me of your dad—and when we met."*

*"Mom?" Izzie said. "You're singing. Again."*

*"I'm sorry, I forgot I can't sing." Her mom said, humming lowly now, her rhythm blowing frosty breath off into the mountains. She looked back toward Izzie. "Oh, so you don't want me to sing, do you? So they can hear me?" her mom pointed to the lift filled with skiers in the car behind them.*

*"Mom, there's a guy, like, my age back there," Izzie said, mortified. "He's kinda cute. Please don't."*

*"You never let me sing," her mom said, laughing. "Someday, you'll wish you had let me sing more."*

Izzie looked thoughtful for a moment and then nodded. "Fine," she said. "Sing as loud as you want. We'll never see them again anyway."

"I wouldn't dream of embarrassing you," her mom said, and dipped her head so that they bumped helmets. "It's just they used to play that song when your dad and I worked here."

"Crazy, isn't it?" her mom said. The ramp was coming up soon. Her mom lifted the plastic shield up and then pulled up the iron bar that they'd rested their boards against.

As they were preparing to unload, her mom looked down at the board strapped to her. Izzie knew the story well. This was the board her dad had bought her mom a long time ago. He gave it to her for Christmas, and then her mom had agreed that it was time to learn to ride. It had blues and greens in a geometric pattern of diamonds and ovals, like some old wallpaper. On the bottom of the board, were the faces of two girls—one white haired, one dark. Her dad had told her mom, "It was the girliest board I could find."

Izzie and Piper slid down the ramp and began to strap in their other boots.

Her mom had never ridden a different snowboard. A couple years back, on one of their family trips, one of the guys on the hotel staff of the Waldorf-Astoria had taken one look at her board and said, "Wow, that's vintage."

Her mom had laughed. "So am I."

She was old. But it was kind of cool that she could snowboard.

Her dad had hugged her mom close as they entered the grand lobby of the hotel behind the cart. "But no less beautiful than the day we met," he said, and kissed her. It embarrassed Izzie to think about them kissing like that in front of all those people. She had been young at the time, *but not too young to realize how gross all that public kissing was.*

*Izzie and her mom stood and headed down a blue trail. Zigzagging down the sparkly snow. It was kind of cool to be one of the first people on the mountain so they could leave the first mark of their snowboard down the groomed hill.*

*Izzie's mom told her just yesterday about how wild her dad had been when they'd met. She'd said his hair was all stand-uppy and white at the tips. Izzie couldn't imagine anything but his short and boring trimmed hairdo when he was on the cover of that business magazine. He was the best CEO or something.*

*But dad never stopped being wild in his heart. That's what mom said, despite his hair looking all neat and trimmed. He was always going on those crazy excursions. Like snowboarding all over mountains where they had to have a helicopter drop them off. And, he had this goal to hike every tall mountain in the world. Her mom said she loved that about him, and she couldn't deny him those trips, even though they always made her sad.*

*After her dad died, her mom spent so much time playing this hauntingly, sad song on her viola. All the time. Her mom played in the viola section for that big orchestra in LA. She taught lessons at the university, too. She wanted to teach Izzie, but she chose the cello instead.*

*"Mom?" Izzie was standing, waiting halfway down the mountain, coming a little more slowly. "Ready?"*

*Piper nodded her head. "Yes, of course. Which way?"*

*Izzie pointed toward the black diamond sign. "Cliffjumper?"*

*Piper shook her head. "No way. Let's take this blue, Meandering Path. It looks familiar somehow."*

Izzie did a little hop on her board to get her going down and waved her hand back. "Okay, I'll follow you. Just try to go a little faster."

They headed down a wide-open area and then her mom veered off to the left. Izzie followed after her. Piper started slowly, her arms hung down while she skirted the narrow trail. When the trail opened up, they finally built up a little speed and carved back and forth, scissoring through the snow.

Izzie and her mom slowed near the edge of the run, where the padded snow had made a little seat.

"Can we sit for a minute? Look, it's a little snow bench."

"Okay, mom," Izzie said, and sat beside her. They fit perfectly and leaned back, her mom wrapped her arms around Izzie. Izzie looked up at the sky where soft snowflakes were twirling down toward her. It was dizzying and beautiful. She couldn't help herself and opened her mouth just slightly, letting a snowflake slip onto her tongue. Her mom was doing the same. But there was something sad in the way she moved, her soft, slow smile. Probably thinking of dad again.

"Mom, don't be so sad."

Her mom looked over, shaking her head. "I'm not sad, I'm happy. I have you." Her mom got a puzzled look on her face and pointed behind Izzie. "Look at that. I think...."

Her mom stood and Izzie followed. She traversed toward the edge, in the roped-off territory.

"Mom, we can't go this way. It's roped off."

Her mom continued riding that direction. "I have to see if it's—"

Izzie followed her mom to a wooden shed; its roof was covered in snow and was surrounded by lots of pine trees and the trees with the eyes. Her mom took her boots out of the bindings and dragged her snowboard behind her.

*She created snow pockets with her boots and then stepped into the waist-deep snow in a little alcove of trees. She tried to push open the door.*

*Izzie took off her own board and began pounding on the door to help. "Mom, can't we get in trouble for this or something?"*

*"I think this is the lift shack where your dad wrote me a poem on the wall."*

*Her mom left her snowboard by a tree before the snow began to get too deep and crawled on her hands and knees to keep her from sinking in. Izzie followed her. It took nearly twenty minutes, and struggling with the door that didn't want to open with all the snow stacked up to it but, finally, after a little pounding and pushing, they were able to wiggle through the sliver of door. Inside, it had trash on the floor and smelled musty, of old wood and a funny kind of stale smoke. She pulled off her gloves and left them on a ledge. There was more writing on the walls, all over everything, and stickers everywhere. But her mom seemed to know right where to go. She went to the back wall and fell to her knees.*

*"I found some poetry scribbled on the wall in here, a long time ago. And I knew it was from your dad. One time when I had to work up here, I added a line of my own to it. I never told him I knew it was his."*

*Izzie saw her mom's tears hitting the harsh, stained wooden floor. Izzie kneeled beside her mom.*

*"Show me."*

*She pointed to the faint words. She whispered them aloud to Izzie.*

> *Love is a secret, snowflakes falling in the dark.*
> *At light, I realize it's covered me.*
> *Swallowed me.*
> *Am I still there when the storm's passed,*
> *after the thaw?*

*Or am I a deadened, frozen remnant of something that
was?
Foreign and new,
re-shaped with you inside me,
frozen in my heart.
Come spring,
from the melted pool,
you're there, living inside my reflected eyes,
looking back at me.*

"That last part. I don't remember it. It's new."

Izzie read the poem again in her head. "Mom, you don't think it could have been from dad?"

Her mom shook her head. "No, no—there's no way it could be. Unless—"

"It looks like the same writing as this," Izzie said, pointing near the top, where the poem began. Izzie knew her dad's handwriting.

***

*H*er mom kept her finger pressed up against the words, indenting the plywood interior. She finally let the tears fall freely.

"It's okay to cry, mom."

And Izzie began to cry too.

After a while, her mom was searching her pocket. "I need a pen." Her mom finally pulled out their car's key. She began carving some letters of her own at the bottom of the poem. It was a laborious process using a key, and even then it came out blocky and barely there.

As she carved, she thought aloud. "It's like the way snowflakes that melt could never re-freeze back into their intricate selves again. He changed me and I could never go back to who I was before I met him. But now, I'm like this *melted, formless puddle on the ground without him here. But I would never have had it any other way."*

*Izzie didn't say anything. She just let her mom say what she needed to. Izzie could feel her dad with them so strongly, she put her hands through the air. As if trying to touch his presence in that tiny shack.*

*Izzie knelt down when her mother stopped carving the key into the wall.*

*She pressed her fingers over the two new words, as if to solidify them onto the end of the poem,*

*Never apart.*

## About Jeana Watters

Jeana Watters is a writer of many things, from newspaper articles and blogs to musical scripts to grocery lists, but she likes writing fiction most of all. Like Piper, she worked as a lift operator in a ski resort to put herself through college and also studied English. A lover of cats, she's glad she has a husband and two daughters to keep her from full crazy-cat-lady status.

She currently lives in Salt Lake City, where she sometimes still rides her vintage 90s Burton Twin snowboard from college. *The Winter's Song* is her second novel.

**Social Media:**

Come find out about my upcoming books and events on my Facebook page:
https://www.facebook.com/jeanawattersbooks

Let's talk books on Instagram:
https://www.instagram.com/hotcocoareads

Find out what books we have in common on Goodreads—and you might as well leave a review for *The Winter's Song* while you're there: www.goodreads.com/jeanaclaudine


**Acknowledgements**:

First and foremost, I want to thank William Shakespeare for writing *The Winter's Tale*, which guided me as I wrote this story. And for all of his plays that pretty much affect most writing as we know it.

I want to thank my daughter, Portia, for putting up with me typing away when she's coming home from school. And to my husband who helps me with scenarios when I'm trying to work through a tricky plot point. And to Bianca, my teenage daughter, for reading my drafts and telling me straight up if my writing is believable to high-school kids.

To my steadfast writing group—Mary, Rachel, Suzanne, Scott, Steve, Randy, Benjamin and Kate—your willingness to read my chapters helped it be what it is. What would I do without your dedication to writing and meeting monthly and all your great ideas when things don't seem quite right in my writing? Oh, and an extra thanks for all the chocolate!

Thanks to my writer-ly friends—Rachel, Christie, Annalisa, Cami—and my mom and sisters, who continue to love and support me and encourage me to just keep writing.

Lastly, thank you to Solstice Publishing for taking a chance on me!

Made in the USA
Middletown, DE
05 August 2019